OUT

Claire Highton - Stevenson

ISBN-13: 978-1546788607

ISBN-10: 1546788603
Facebook: @Claire Highton-Stevenson

Twitter: @ItsClaStevOfficial

Cover Credit: Claire Stevenson Photography

DEDICATION

For my wife, Louise, the wind beneath my wings. Without whom I wouldn't be able to spend all these hours writing down my imagination.

For Mum and Dad... A love story to remember.

ACKNOWLEDGMENTS

This book would not have been possible without the support and help from many people. However, special thanks goes out to:

Michelle Arnold, whose continuous encouragement kept me going. For the hours of proof reading and education.

Kelly Daniel, whose knowledge of medical procedures and treatments made it possible for me to write anything that made sense.

Chris and Niall, whose support and encouragement means the world. Not to mention they have office building skills!

.

<u>Part One</u>

Claire Highton-Stevenson

Chapter One

The echoes of climax shuddered through the closed door as one solitary tear slid slowly down Cam's cheek. Time stalled, an abrupt halt as sounds of giggling erupted from Jessica. The bed frame squeaked as bodies moved and changed positions; everything was loud and clear as it resonated through the wall. Their betrayal.

~Out~

It had been one of those days. The ones where anything that can go wrong, will go wrong, and Camryn Thomas was resigned to just deal with it as best she could. Pollards department store was not where she wanted to be right now, but with very little choice in the matter, she plodded on regardless.

The store, as usual at this time of year, was filled to the brim with everything anyone could possibly ever need at Christmas, aisles and aisles of festive absolutes that would be used once and promptly forgotten before New Year. The lights dazzled and the cheery seasonal songs played merrily in the background persuading everyone that they were just *so* happy to be there, and that included Camryn Thomas on any other day but today.

She hadn't felt at all well that morning, but what with it being Christmas, she couldn't afford to take the day off. So, she was dosed up on every over the counter medication she could get her hands on in the hope that at some point she would feel even the teeniest bit better. Of course, that wasn't to be and by midday she was worse than ever.

Her boss Malcolm, the ever-present miserable sod that he was, had finally given in and taken pity on her, sending her home early. His concerns were purely selfish – he didn't want it, but she didn't care and she took the opportunity she was presented with, with both hands, snotty tissues and all.

She waited patiently at the bus stop not particularly caring which one she got on at this point, she was cold and her head hurt in more places than she thought was possible. When the right bus finally did arrive, she clambered on, flashed her oyster card and sank down into the well-worn tartan seat and closed her eyes.

She was nudged from her resting by an older lady flopping down in the empty seat next to her, her bulky clothing causing her to land half in Cam's lap. The woman looked decidedly like she was off out on a trip to the Arctic Circle, rather than a ride on the 143 bus up the high street. Wrapped in a beige overcoat that was far too big for her, a hat covered her grey curls, while a scarf was wound so tight around her face that Cam seriously wanted to check she could actually breathe underneath it all. At least she didn't smell, or worse still, itch. That would have been just Cam's luck.

She let her head fall heavily against the cool window and closed her eyes again, focusing only on her own breathing, mainly through the one nostril however, as the other was so blocked it had given her a headache. Her breathing alternating between either nostril, dependant on which way her head tilted. Right now it was the left that was clearer and so she quickly shoved the nasal inhaler up the right nostril and sniffed loudly. The old woman looked around for another seat and sighed heavily; the bus was packed and she was stuck next to the germ spreader.

The desire to just get home was overwhelming. Maybe she could have a hot steaming bath, sweat out some of these germs. Then she would make a hot toddy and climb into bed with Jessica, well that was once Jess came home of course; until then she would probably lie on the sofa feeling sorry for herself.

After what felt like a lifetime, the bus reached her stop. Dislodging the old woman from her seat in order to pass her, she ignored the grumbled mutterings and was at the doors before they were even open. Lurching off, she begin the long trudge up the slippery hill to their flat.

It was a vicious wind whipping around her face, and her already red nose began to feel more like frostbite was settling in for the duration. The constant rubbing with a tissue had meant that she was rocking a very festive Rudolph look. Past caring now, she trekked onwards.

Dark grey clouds threatened a snow storm, and the winter gloom was soon approaching. Normally she didn't mind a cold winter evening; it made for some excellent snuggling time. It meant warm jumpers and cosy blankets, hot chocolate and old black and white movies...but not when she felt like death itself.

~Out~

Other than the evil cold she was suffering with, life was just about perfect though, and now she and her girlfriend would be spending Christmas together and unwrapping the presents that were already piling up under the tree. Every bauble and fairy light she had hung around the tree had made her smile. Jess would be so excited when she finally got to open all the gifts. Cam had worked hard to save a little here and a little there in order to buy Jess some decent presents and not just the crap they sold at Pollards.

She had been living with Jessica for just over six months now and she couldn't have been happier about it. Ready to be in a permanent relationship, she wanted to be a grown-up at last and no longer had any interest in sleeping around or playing the field; not that she had done very much of that anyway. In Jess, it seemed as though she had found the perfect partner.

Her parents, on the other hand, hadn't quite been so happy about her 'choice' of partner, but that was their issue because in truth, they were not going to be happy with anyone Cam chose, simply because she would be female. She didn't care about that much now either; it had bothered her through her teens and most of her twenties, but now...not so much.

The key slid easily into the lock. She opened the door and was struck by one of two things. Firstly, it was warm, and secondly, she could hear voices. She felt the radiator in the hallway by the door with her palm - it was hot to the touch. Muttering to herself about Jess forgetting to turn it off, she shrugged off her coat and hung it on the hook nearest to her. Under the circumstances, she was pretty relieved that it was nice and warm inside; maybe just this once she could forgive her lover and her constant money-wasting ways.

Her biggest concern right now was the muffled voices she could hear. Her first thought was maybe Jess had left the TV on too, but that really wasn't likely as Jess rarely put the TV on in the morning, she was a radio girl. So it bothered her as

8

she went about undressing. The hat stand stood stoically just inside the door and like it always did, her hat joined her jacket on the hook before she then slipped her socked feet out of her trainers, leaving them neatly on the shoe rack as she picked up the mail from the mat and begun to head further into the flat.

The flat wasn't very big; a short hallway that held all the doors was barely ten feet long. Flicking through the mail, she sorted the envelopes into two piles while she wandered down the brightly painted passage to the bedroom, intent on stripping out of the rest of her clothes and heading straight to the bathroom for that promised bath.

As she passed the lounge, she realised in an instant that the muffled sounds were definitely not coming from the TV. The television was clearly switched off. They were coming from further up the hallway, from their bedroom - but they didn't have a TV in their bedroom. She frowned, completely perplexed and a little worried. What if it was burglars? But that fear was soon quashed.

Drawing nearer, the muffled sounds became clearer and a nauseating feeling clung to her guts as they roiled.

Optimistically, she tried to convince herself that it was just Jess shirking off work for the day. She almost sniggered at the prospect of catching her girlfriend pleasuring herself on a sneaky day off. That was until she heard the subsequent sound – and that definitely wasn't Jessica! Her heart raced and her mouth parched as her breath caught in her chest. The gut-wrenching churning enveloped her stomach once more. The tightness in her throat around the sudden lump that had appeared and couldn't be swallowed down was almost suffocating her.

Standing outside of the bedroom door listening, trying desperately to think of any other reason why those sounds were coming from her girlfriend behind the flimsy door. She had almost convinced herself that it was all just innocent, but once she heard the other voice moan and then utter that solitary word, '*Please*', she knew there and then that it was anything but innocent. She knew that voice too well and she couldn't believe it, she wouldn't believe it, not until she saw with her own eyes because there was no way on this Earth that the person who that voice belonged to would be in her bedroom with her girlfriend having sex! No fucking way. It was one thing a girlfriend cheating on you, but your best friend too? No, Kate just wouldn't do such a thing.

They had been best friends since meeting in the first year of secondary school. As eleven-year-olds they were scrawny, naïve new starters who had instantly sparked off one another and became firm best friends. Kate was straight for fuck's sake!

She wiped at her cheek, knowing she had a choice now: back out of the flat, pretend she hadn't heard anything, and slowly let the knowledge eat away at her until it destroyed their relationships anyway; or take the initiative and seize back the control in her life that was slowly slipping from her grasp, discover once and for all what was going on behind that closed door between her lover and her best friend.

Decision made Cam reached out hesitantly for the door handle, fingers trembling. She wavered, not wanting to touch it, knowing once she did then there was no going back, no way to *un-see* it. But she had to do it, because Camryn Thomas was nobody's doormat.

Like the wheels of justice, the doorknob turned slowly. She made no sound, but for the beating of her own heart that rapped out a cadence so loud she thought she would be heard instantly. The door glided open as wide as it would go, a silent accomplice to her detecting skills.

The room was in darkness, almost. The curtains were still drawn with just the bedside lamp to illuminate the events in front of her as she witnessed the definitive betrayal. On top of the pink and white duvet – the one they had bought together in the first week they moved here – on her fucking bed lay her girlfriend. She was naked, legs spread wide with her best friend knelt neatly between them, her torso bent low, long black hair tossed to one side. It was pretty clear what she was doing.

Time stopped. It felt like she stood there for hours just watching the repugnant scene play out in front of her, images that not once in her worst nightmares did she ever consider would become her reality. The hurt that rushed through her in that moment was heated and angry, a raw and open wound. She couldn't find the words; all she could do was stand there staring and wait, feeling sick to her stomach and immobile.

It took several seconds before Jessica threw her head sideways in the midst of her impending orgasm and opened her eyes. Like a startled rabbit, her senses refocused the instant she recognised Camryn standing there in the doorway. Her hand slowly lowered and pushed Kate away.

Kate's eyes rose from their concentrated glazed stare, a questioning frown on her face. It didn't take long for her brain to register the same startled gape as she looked straight into the pain-stricken, glowering eyes of her friend. Her best friend.

"Oh my god, Camryn, it's not...It's not what you think." She desperately tried to explain, to find the words that would make this nightmare stop and change the outcome from what she knew was coming. Grabbing a sheet, she pulled it up quickly to cover her nakedness. She looked so pitiful that for a mere second in time Camryn actually felt sorry for her. She gave herself a mental slap. There was no room for sympathy, not with such betrayal lying on the bed.

"Really Kate? What exactly do you think I think it is?" Her voice was calm, surprisingly. Jess was still yet to move, she hadn't even attempted to cover herself. Her body was still flushed and sweaty from the exploits of just minutes earlier. She just lay there staring at the ceiling as her mind whirred into action to come up with the reasons why Cam should be ok with this.

"Yes, ok I mean it is, it looks like what you think it is, but—" Kate rambled on sheepishly, climbing off the bed and reaching for her clothes. She hopped about on one leg, then the other as she desperately tried to get herself decent; she looked back and forth between her best friend and the woman on the bed.

"But what? You just popped round to see me, even though you're fully aware I would be at work and what? You fell head first into my girlfriends naked—" She was going to use the C-word, a word she hated. On any other given day it wouldn't even enter her head to use it, but on this occasion it felt quite apt; it was aggressive and said exactly what she was feeling. But she refrained, refusing to drop to their level. "Is that what happened? It was an accident? You tripped and landed on my fucking bed!" she cried, her anger finally pushing through the coldness. "At the exact same moment as my naked girlfriend opened her legs? Is that what you're going with?" Cam was livid now, the anger coursing through her. Actually, livid was an understatement. She was *incensed* that even when caught red-handed, Kate was choosing bullshit over an explanation, an apology even.

"Cam please, can we talk—"

"Just get out, get out Kate." Cam was numb, her emotions had switched off. She couldn't afford to be emotional, to let them see what they had done, how they were destroying her. No, they wouldn't get to see that, to take that from her.

Kate turned to Jessica, silently pleading with her to do something, anything, but she just sat there avoiding eye contact. "Are you going to tell her?" Kate, her one time best friend, screeched at her so-called lover. With no response from Jessica, all Kate had left to do was finish getting dressed and get out of there and hope to god she could salvage something from this at a later point, explain the situation to Cam and deal with the fallout being truthful would bring. In her heart and mind, though, she knew already that she had lost everything.

With Kate out of the room, Jessica sat up and leisurely pulled her T-shirt over her head. There was just one tiny simple word that said all Cam needed to say. "Why?" Cam whispered. Her hands raked through her blonde hair and she slumped lethargically against the wall waiting for the answer that she already knew wouldn't be good enough.

Jessica finally had the good grace to at least appear sorry. Although now, instead of staring at the ceiling she stared at the floor, unable to look Cam in the eye. She took her time to think about her reply, the silence creating a tension that was tangible to both woman for very different reasons.

Standing, Jess made her way across the room to retrieve her underwear. "I don't know why, she isn't even my type, but I was attracted to her and she was attracted to me, she begged me and I--"

"She's fucking straight!" Cam screeched at her.

"Maybe so, but that doesn't change that she was, or is, attracted to me and that we decided to fuck and just get it out of our systems." For someone literally just caught with her pants down, Jessica was extremely calm, and that pissed Camryn off even more.

Cam nodded her head. "I see, and how many others have you just fucked to get it out of your system? Is this a regular thing? Do all my friends just pop round when I'm not here?" Her sarcastic comment received a roll of Jessica's eyes at her. "My best fucking friend Jess!!" she yelled, her fists balling subconsciously.

"I know Camryn and I'm sorry. I really am, it was a mistake, we—" There was a pause as she took a moment. "We clearly weren't thinking with our heads...or our hearts," she said honestly, finally really looking at her girlfriend. "I love you Cam." She sounded so sincere when she said it and Cam had no doubt she thought she believed it, but how could she? How could she really love anyone when she could so easily break the heart she had made promises to safeguard?

Cam raised her hands in defeat as she moved forwards and reached for the suitcase that was perched precariously on top of the wardrobe. Tossing it on the bed, she noticed it still had the airport baggage stickers from their last trip, a long weekend in Rome. It had been romantic and had made Cam consider maybe one day they might even get married and have their honeymoon there. Not now though.

"What are you doing?" Finally the realisation of what she had done and the fallout from it was sinking in. Cam was leaving her. It was unthinkable; she couldn't just leave her. This wasn't what was supposed to happen. Kate was just a bit of fun, but Camryn, she was the one. She moved swiftly to stand close to her lover, to reach out to her, but pulled back at the last moment when Cam's face dared her to continue.

Throwing her clothes into the case without any real care, she reached down, snatched her holdall from under the bed, and began walking around the flat snatching things she wasn't prepared to leave behind: Jess followed her in and out of rooms trying to stop her from picking things up, but Cam was determined. There was no coming back.

"No, Cam wait, please." She reached out and placed a hand on her arm, but the blonde shrugged it off. "You can't just leave me!" Jessica pleaded. She stood there, her light brown hair messy and tousled, green eyes glistening with tears that threatened, but never quite managed, to fall. That was all the clarity Cam needed. Everything with Jess was '*almost*'. She had clearly been so wrong in her assessment that their relationship had been 'the one'. Cam shrugged her off once more and shook her head.

"Camryn please, we can talk about this, work it out. It will never happen again I swear to you," Jessica promised solemnly as she followed Camryn back into the bedroom and watched as she continued to throw things into the bag.

"It shouldn't have happened this time." She regarded the bed and then sneered. "You made it, now you can lie in it. I don't care who with anymore."

"You don't mean that! You said you loved me. You can't just stop," she screeched at her back. "I won't let you just leave me Camryn."

"You can't stop me!" She turned away again, but Jessica grabbed her shoulder this time and spun her back around.

"*You* don't walk away from me," she hissed, her fingers tightening their grip on her arm. Cam tried to shrug her off, but she held tight. "You'll regret it." She held her gaze and then as though nothing had happened, she smiled and released her. It sent a cold shiver down Cam's spine.

Ignoring her, Cam zipped up the suitcase and slung the bag over her shoulder. She wheeled her baggage down the hall to the door where she slipped her trainers back on her feet and pulled her jacket from the hook.

She stopped as her hand reached for the doorknob, and Jessica thought for a fleeting second that maybe she had changed her mind, but as she crept closer she could see Cam was fiddling with something in her hand. When she turned back to Jessica, she held out a small shiny object between her fingers.

"I won't need this anymore," she said as she placed her key in Jessica's palm. "Goodbye Jessica." With that said, she left. Dragging her case and bag down the stairs to the communal entrance, the finality of it all hit home. As she slid down the paint flaked wall, her arse landing on the cold concrete step, she let herself grieve the loss. And when the final sob left her chest, she stood, determined to face the world and whatever else it had to throw at her. Things would change, go her way, she was sure of it.

Chapter Two

It was May, the sun was shining, and it was hot. Hotter than any other day so far. The land of dreams was in the middle of an unexpected heat wave.

Since arriving in Los Angeles, Camryn Thomas had never felt better. She had come a long way in the last few months and now, as she walked around the building she was interested in, she couldn't help but grin to herself.

Those first few weeks following her break up with Jessica and the discovery that her best friend was nothing more than a treacherous rat were difficult, to say the least. Not only did she lose the two most important people in her life, but she also had to find somewhere else to live, and there weren't many options for someone with barely any savings. Deposits and rents had to be paid in advance; it was all just way too much. She did consider going back to her parents, but she quickly dismissed that idea when she reminded herself what kind of man her father was nowadays. So, she ended up renting a room with a bunch of students. It was a cold and damp room. Everything she owned tainted in a musty mildew stench, but it had a bed and right then, that was all she had needed.

She stood on the spot and spun around slowly in a circle, reminded of those dark days, as she took everything in. The old paintwork flaked in places. The carpets reeked with the stench of spilt drinks and dust. The place hadn't been cleaned in years; that much was obvious. It was nothing like the plush hotel suite she was staying in at the Ritz Carlton, with its huge bed and marbled bathroom. She had never slept

18

anywhere, so comfortable in her life...and then there was Amanda.

She hung her head subconsciously when she thought of Amanda. The day she had arrived in LA and met Amanda would be forever burnt into her memory as another reminder of what not to do!

"Good afternoon, do you have a reservation with us today?" the chirpy brunette on the front desk asked as Camryn strolled up.

"Uh, no, I-."

"That won't be a problem, may I take some details?" She dazzled. That was how Cam would describe her when she smiled.

"Sure." Cam rattled off the answers to all the questions she asked and took the opportunity to really look around her as the brunette, whom she had now discovered was called Amanda, checked her system for a free room.

The reception area was a bright and airy space without being too flashy. Cam liked it. The staff looked smart and professional in their uniforms, especially Amanda. She appraised the woman on the opposite side of the desk. Her jacket and skirt fit her perfectly, accentuating every curve. She was hot, and somebody Cam would probably have said was out of her league in her previous life, but not now.

"Ms Thomas, we have three options for you today. The executive guest room, the junior suite, or the executive suite." She blushed slightly when she looked up and caught the blonde English woman giving her the once over.

"Ok, I really don't know what the difference is, but I think

a suite sounds nice, don't you?" She held her gaze. "I am not sure how long I will be staying though. Does that make a difference?" Cam leant forward, one arm resting on the countertop, smiling.

The brunette eyed her up and down, obviously considering whether this woman in a t-shirt and combats with just two small cases could actually afford the rooms available. Cam pulled her new gold card from her wallet and placed it on the desk between them.

"Money isn't the problem," the blonde whispered, holding her gaze once more. "I'll take the executive suite for a month and then we can see what I will want to do after that. Will that work for you?"

Amanda dazzled, still holding Cam's gaze. She licked her lower lip and then caught it between her teeth. "I think that would be perfect, and if there is anything else I can do to help make your stay with us more comfortable Ms Thomas, please do not hesitate to call me." Flirting? Cam could do flirting.

"Oh, I will be sure to do exactly that Amanda. Tell me, is there anywhere I can grab something to eat?!" She continued to lean toward the attractive brunette. The beautiful receptionist faltered just slightly as she was inputting the details of Cam's stay.

"Uh, well the restaurant here is very good." Amanda passed an electronic key card across the desk. Her eyes roamed Cam's face.

"Maybe you could show me later, when you get off work?" Cam suggested, her fingers ghosting over the receptionist's to take the card.

"I would be delighted." She dazzled one more time. *"Glen will show you to your room."* She switched her attention to Glen and instructed him to take the customer's bags to the penthouse. *"Enjoy your stay."*

And that was exactly what she did.

The building was going to need a lot of work, that much was obvious, but it wasn't anything that she could foresee as being a problem. She was already in touch with some good construction guys. The bar area wasn't too bad, plenty to work with once they got rid of all the old cracked mirrors and posters advertising 'party nights' from a long time ago.

She thought back to that morning, when she had woken up with Amanda's sweet smile. She would spend a lifetime hating herself for the way she managed to knock that from her beautiful face.

"I'm off all day today, did you want to do something together?" Amanda asked. *She was sitting in front of the dresser's huge mirror combing through her long hair. The towel she had been wrapped in hung loosely and her naked body was almost on full display. She didn't seem to mind and neither did Cam, not about the nakedness anyway. She had certainly seen enough of it these past couple of months.*

"Uh, actually I have some business to attend to today," she remarked, checking her phone for a message she was expecting.

"Oh." The dark-haired woman stopped all movement and observed the blonde via the mirror. *"Well, dinner then? I was thinking maybe we could meet my friends for drinks later."*

"I'd rather not if you don't mind," Cam said. She stepped in closer and rested her palms on the woman's bare shoulders, kissing her cheek. *"Listen, I've bought a house so I'm not going to*

be here for much longer," she added, as if that explained everything. Amanda remained still, her features frowning as she considered Cam's words.

"I see. So, you're too busy to meet my friends later because you're buying a house today?"

"No, the house is done, I am buying a club today," she announced as though it were obvious.

"Ok, a club? You didn't tell me. Should we not talk about these things?" Now it was Cam's turn to be perplexed. She realised as she continued to move around the room getting ready that maybe there were some things they should have discussed. Moving across the room, she sat on the bed behind Amanda. Turning her around to face her, she took hold of the towel and moved it back in place to cover her up.

"Amanda, you are a beautiful, fun and wonderful young woman and under other circumstances things between us might be different but—"

"Oh God, you're breaking up with me?" She tugged the towel tighter. Her face flushed and tears began to well.

"What? Look...I should have been more forthright from the beginning, I thought we were on the same page, but I see now that...I'm sorry, but I just don't want to be in a relationship. I thought you understood that this was just fun and that—" She didn't get a chance to finish before she felt the harsh sting of a palm slapping her cheek.

"Fun! That's all I am? Two months of fucking me and all I am is fun?" She stood and grabbed her clothes from the floor where they had landed the previous night. "Fuck you Cam."

It was a lesson learnt the hard way and a mistake Cam would not make again. The last thing she ever intended was to hurt someone else. From now on she would be upfront from the very start with any potential date, that it would be one date and one date only.

"So, Ms Thomas, what do we think?" Her real estate guy, Calvin Jacobs, stood in front of her smiling, breaking her from her thoughts. He tried to dazzle too.

"I think...that for the right price I would be very interested, *at the right price.*" She returned his smile. She might be rich now, but she wasn't going to just throw money away for the sake of it. "I need to completely gut and remodel the entire place, new lighting and electrics; it's going to take a lot of work."

"Sure, and I can guarantee that the owner is happy to do a deal here."

"Good. So, let's quit playing around. My offer is 1.8 *if* we do the deal today and everything is signed and sealed by the end of the month."

His grin widened as he mentally calculated the fee he would earn from this deal. He had already upgraded his own apartment from the tidy sum he had earned from Cam's beach house. "Let me make a call."

She watched him walk outside as she chuckled to herself. She had just offered 1.8 million dollars for a building she intended to turn into the biggest and most exclusive gay bar in Los Angeles. She, Camryn Thomas from the council estates of Southeast London could and would now do whatever the hell she wanted.

"Just those please," she had said. The man behind the counter smiled at her. She thought she remembered him saying his name was Javid, but she couldn't be sure so, she just smiled back. Sometimes, she thought he might be the friendliest face she

saw each day.

"Late night?" he asked. Cam was grateful for his interest. Her friends no longer called to check on her. They thought she'd had enough time to 'get over it,' and she didn't like to be a whiner about it.

"Yes, but I get to have a lay in tomorrow so not too bad." She picked up a bar of chocolate from the display on the counter, "And this too please."

"Can I interest you in a lottery ticket?" he asked, pointing to the sign that advertised the Euro Millions Lottery and its headline of 'jackpot rollover expected prize £95m.'

"Well I don't normally but, oh what the hell, got to be in it to win it right?" she laughed as he printed off her ticket. She pushed the pink ticket into her purse along with her change and grabbed the carrier bag that the store clerk had packed her items in for her.

"Good luck!" he said, with a wave and another smile.

"Thank you, I could really do with some of that. Good night."

~Out~

By the time Saturday came around she had forgotten all about her ticket. It was only while lying in bed with a cup of tea and some toast, flicking through the news headlines on her smartphone, that she realised the draw had been the night before.

Headline: One winner. UK. The idea of winning that sum of money filtered through her imagination and was gone in a *second. She just wasn't that lucky, but there were other prizes to be won. It wasn't all about the big jackpot.*

With that thought she got up from the warmth of her bed. It was the warmest place in the house. Her room was so cold that there was condensation on the outside of the windows. Pulling her purse from her bag, she opened it and found her ticket. She hoped maybe she might win a small prize that would pay for her deposit a bit sooner! One could only hope. A few thousand pounds would be good right now.

Googling the winning numbers on her phone as she unfolded the pink ticket, she studied the numbers that had been randomly generated by the machine, noting that one was her birthdate. It took her a moment of flicking back and forth to find the numbers she was looking for as there were several draws and different types of Lotto that were done each week. When she finally got the ones she needed, she almost fainted.

She stared at the brightly lit screen for what felt like an eternity, but in actuality it was just six minutes. Six minutes of absolute disbelief. Six minutes of checking and rechecking that her ticket did in fact have the same numbers on it. Her brain was trying to process what that meant. Because it just wasn't possible that she was the winner; that was something that happened to other people. You read about them in the papers.

But the ticket couldn't lie, could it? It couldn't change the numbers? The numbers were there in black and white. She was the owner of the ticket that had won over 95 million pounds.

"Ms Thomas?" The voice came from behind her. Turning, she found Calvin grinning his trademark beam. "We have a deal." She returned his grin and they shook on it. She now owned a derelict nightclub.

As they were leaving the building, she noticed a woman with pink coloured hair trying to catch a glimpse through the open doorway. She wore her clothing the same way she wore her hair: messy and bright!

"Can I help you?" Cam asked. Since arriving in LA she had accepted quite quickly that this was a diverse place to be. It was one of the reasons she had settled in so quickly.

"Oh, hey...sorry, I was just being nosey. I used to work here." She held out a hand. "Erin, Erin Donald." Calvin looked bored; he clearly had somewhere else to be, but Cam didn't. In fact, now that Amanda wouldn't be waiting for her, she had the entire afternoon to herself.

"Thank you, Calvin. I'll speak to you soon." She dismissed him, giving him the out he needed to politely walk away. "So, Erin? What did you do here?"

"I worked the bar. Four or five nights a week." There was a coffee shop across the road from them. The prospect of speaking with someone who knew the business and what kind of clientele had been using the place was an opportunity she didn't want to lose.

"Wanna grab a coffee? I'm buying the building and would love to hear your opinion on the business."

"It was a long time ago but, sure, why not?"

Chapter Three

One year later and OUT had been open for almost six months. Totally renovated from top to bottom, the club had been gradually gaining attention from the West Hollywood crowd and was now definitely on the map as one of *the* places to be seen and hang out in WeHo.

Visa issues had meant that for the first few months of her stay in LA, she had had to keep flying back and forth to the UK or Europe. So, she used her time wisely and started investing. There was a bar she used to use in London that had come up for sale and so she bought it; setting up a management team to run it seemed sensible. She also bought herself a luxury apartment overlooking the Thames; it made sense as a further investment and also gave her a base to stay whenever she was forced back to London. Her portfolio of property and business investments grew rapidly.

Now, she wasn't just spending, she was earning.

~Out~

It was August, and it was hot – the kind of heat Cam had felt on that day the previous year when she had bought the business. She had not long ago celebrated her 35th birthday, which had been fun, a lot of fun! A group of Swedish tourists had been partying down on Venice Beach and somehow or other Cam, along with Erin, had found themselves invited to join the girls as they enjoyed the sunshine. In all honesty, her birthday weekend was no different to any other weekend. She went out, had fun, and took a woman home. That was her life in LA: nothing serious except for the business. Nothing complicated and no strings attached. Ingrid and Ursula understood completely.

Did it get any better than this? She guessed it could, but if it didn't then she would still die a happy woman.

~Out~

Arriving at the club the following Saturday night on her Yamaha, she noted the stares of folk as they stood outside queueing to get in. The machine was red, big and powerful, and she loved it as she roared through the parking lot and set it on its stand in her own personal parking space. She also had to admit it was somewhat of a chick magnet. Not that she had much trouble pulling the ladies as it was, but when she arrived on the bike wearing her leathers, they fell over themselves to talk to her. Some just downright propositioned her. It had been the most sexually fulfilling year of her life so far too. She had arrived in a new town, found her footing, and enjoyed every minute of it.

On this occasion, like many others in the past, she had a passenger: Lauren was tall, blonde, and typical Hollywood. Dating for Cam was fun. She respected each of them and never ever treated anyone unkindly or unfairly, but she made one thing clear to all of them, Lauren included, that no matter how great a time they had (and they had had a great time!), she wouldn't be seeing them again. Not in a dating capacity anyway. It wasn't that she didn't like them, just that she wasn't prepared to share her heart with anyone again. They could have fun and enjoy each other's company, but that was all she had to offer. There would be no more Amandas on her conscience.

Pulling off her helmet, she held still on the bike so Lauren could climb off safely. As Lauren took her own helmet off, her long, flowing, fair hair fell around her face like a Charlie's Angel.

"Thanks for a great night Cam, you sure you don't wanna do it again?" she said, her deep Texas accent lingering in Cam's ears as she leant forward and placed a gentle kiss just below her ear.

"You know the rules Lauren." Lauren was gorgeous, and another night with her wouldn't be that awful an option, but she knew the perils of allowing things to drag on. Amanda was always on her mind. She didn't want to hurt anyone else like that.

"It was worth a try." The Texan smiled, then kissed her for the last time before she ambled away with a little wave of her fingers over her shoulder.

Cam watched her go and chuckled to herself. She was hot. There was no doubt about that.

~Out~

Since arriving in California, she had also taken to using a personal trainer. Trent had pushed her physique to its limits. Her body, though always quite slim, was now defined and toned in all the right places. She drew glances from men and woman alike. Every muscle and sinew was worked to its fullest potential and she enjoyed every bit of the attention that it got her.

By Hollywood standards she wasn't what you would declare a beautiful woman, but she certainly was pretty and had been told on numerous occasions that her eyes were what won it for her: big and blue, ice blue in some lights. When Camryn Thomas looked at you, you felt it. Her smile definitely enhanced the experience; it lit up her face as she smiled with her cheeks, dimples and all.

Her style was simple. She kept her long hair and it had gotten even blonder from living in such a sunny climate like California. At almost six feet tall, she was an impressive sight, and with time had grown a confidence that she had previously lacked. Gone was the unsure Camryn who would settle. Now she was self-assured; her self-esteem had rocketed with the time and effort she had spent on looking her best. She wasn't vain, but she now understood her attributes and made the best of them. Having the finances to enjoy it all without fear of how the next bill would be paid was always an advantage.

To look at her, you would never assume she had so many millions in the bank, and she liked it that way. She wanted to be liked for who she was rather than how much money she had. She never talked about it. Of course, her staff at the bar knew she had money. You didn't get to own a bar like this without having some financial clout to back it up. They just had no idea how much or where it came from, and they never asked about it either.

~Out~

Stripping out of her leathers, she was ready to enjoy the best and busiest night of the week.

"Hey Cam," Erin called out in greeting above the pounding beat of the bass that pumped through the sound system – a system that would keep the throngs of hot, sweaty men and women grinding and writhing on the dance floor into

30

the small hours. Although it was predominantly a lesbian bar, there were no steadfast rules about whether men could come in or even if you had to be gay. So long as everyone respected each other then all was good with the world according to Cam and her positive outlook. So far they had had little trouble for Gavin to deal with, just the odd drunk and one drug-related incident, which was the one thing Cam would not tolerate. Gavin Grogan was in charge of a very small security team that had her full support in dealing with anything untoward.

Erin Donald had become Camryn's right-hand woman virtually overnight when it came to running the bar; although not officially the manager, she might as well have been, and Camryn treated her as such. She planned to make it official as soon as she got the chance to talk to Erin. She had proven herself over and over already, and Cam was finally ready to put her trust in her and let her run OUT fulltime. She didn't look like your typical bar manager with her purple hair and the wacky clothes she liked to wear, but Cam liked that. She liked it when women could just be themselves, live their lives how they chose to.

Nothing got past Erin when it came to keeping the bar running smoothly. She was on top of her game, the staff respected her, and the clients knew not to push their luck. Cam could come and go and knew that if ever there was a problem, either Erin or Gavin would deal with it.

"Hi Erin. Any problems I need to know about?" Cam asked, her English accent still very much intact.

"Only that Jenny called in sick *again*," she said with a sigh. "Apparently she spent the night puking." She shrugged her shoulders. "Who knows, but we're one down behind the bar so, any chance you can help out?" She always asked politely, but in reality she was just telling her she was working.

"Sure thing! Just let me take my stuff upstairs to the office and I'm good to go," Cam told her as she climbed the stairs two at a time, her long legs enjoying the stretch. She threw her gear down on the small settee and whipped off her top, replacing it with the uniform T-shirt embroidered with the word OUT in rainbow stitching on the left breast pocket, and headed back down to the bar.

By 9 p.m. the bar was pretty busy, but nothing like it was going to be in an hour or so. Cam liked this time best. Being busy but having enough time to chat with the regulars a little always left her in a good mood, and this night was no different.

"You know Cam, I was thinking, if I had multiple personalities, would that mean each one could go on a date with you and not break your one date rule?" laughed Angie, a short haired femme brunette Cam had bedded the previous year when she had first arrived in LA. They had had a great night together and then met again when Cam opened the doors to OUT. Angie was one of her first customers, and they had struck up a friendship that was as close as she was going to have with anyone.

"Hmm, I'd have to think about that, but I guess it would depend on if I was attracted to your other personalities, I mean what if one was called Dick?" the bar owner giggled. She never got annoyed with Angie and her constant flirting; she knew the score and though she would always play up to Cam, she respected her honesty and her rules. She was also one of the only people who knew Camryn had been hurt by someone back home. Although she didn't know all of the details, she knew it had been painful and that Cam didn't want to talk about it.

As they were bantering back and forth, Cam spotted a woman hovering near the entrance, clearly unsure whether to enter or to leave as fast as she could. Watching the woman, Cam was intrigued to see what the outcome of the dilemma would be. She saw it often: people trying to decide whether today was going to be the day they were going to be brave enough or not, the culmination of hours of thought and discussions in their own heads as to whether they can really be the person they were born to be. It was something that annoyed Cam a lot, that in this day and age, in a town as diverse as LA, people were still afraid to come out and just be who they wanted to be. Or, it could just be someone who had no idea where she was and just wanted a drink, but she didn't think so.

Chapter Four

She was tall, athletic, and brunette, definitely brunette, but that was all Cam could discern from her outward appearance. She was wearing white linen trousers that were tailored to the waist but flared a little on their way down to the floor, and it was a long way down. A black shirt buttoned up the middle and tucked inside the waistband of the trousers billowed slightly, and a baseball cap kept all those curls off her face. She kept her head down somewhat, so Cam couldn't really gauge what the outcome might be by her facial inflections. She watched her though, as she hopped back and forth from one foot to the other nervously, hands firmly in her pockets, making her shoulders hunch.

At last, she made a decision and slowly edged her way through the crowd to the bar. As she sat on the first stool she came to, Cam could see that she really was an incredibly beautiful woman. Her mane of black curls was tied back into a tidy ponytail and tucked through the back of the cap, and she had the warmest brown eyes Cam had ever seen. She was wearing very little make up, but she really didn't need it; she was clearly just beautiful. Nervous as hell, but beautiful all the same. Her cheekbones were chiselled, the line of her nose just right. With her tanned and glowing skin tone, she was not the kind of woman to be ignored, and yet she was hiding out under a cap.

"Hi, what can I get ya?" Cam shouted above the noise, drawing the woman's attention. She smiled in an attempt to put her at ease a little and received a small upward turn of lips in return. *Wow, dimples.*

"Um, just a beer. Thank you," she answered. Her voice was a little husky, like she had smoked twenty Marlboros a day for the last fifteen years. *Sexy.*

Apparently no matter where you went in the world, the English accent was appreciated by most, and Cam had always taken advantage of it. Now though, as she listened to the women in front of her she finally got it.

"Beer? You don't strike me as a beer drinker." Cam took a few seconds to study her some more.

"No? What makes you think that?" There was mirth in her words. Her smile widened, causing the corners of her eyes to crease.

"Far too classy for beer but, if it's a beer that you want, it's a beer you shall have!" She grabbed a cold bottle from the fridge, uncapped it and passed it across. "First one's on the house," she beamed. A flirtatious wink thrown in the brunette's direction wouldn't hurt, and with that she turned back to Angie and her date, Fran, all the while keeping one eye on the gorgeous woman sitting alone at the bar by herself a few feet away. She wondered if this was the first time this woman had ever been in a gay bar or even if she realised it was one. It wasn't like the bar was painted pink with rainbows sprouting out of the roof and a giant arrow pointing 'the queers to here!'

In fact, it had a rather stylish and modern décor. Lots of mirrors had once adorned the walls, along with posters and garish paint colours. Now, though, it was subtle and allowed the eye to be drawn further in rather than make you want to wear sunglasses inside. It was dark. What kind of dance area worked in a bright environment? None! So the lighting had been adapted and created to make sure everything complemented everything else and created a welcoming place to come and dance, flirt, and play.

Noticing her beer was almost finished, Cam brought a fresh one to her. "You look like you're ready for another?" The woman smiled, tilting her head in acquiescence. She was exceptionally good looking, but there was something more that Cam couldn't quite put her finger on. "I'm Cam by the way," she told her as she leant forward, her forearms on the bar with her hands subconsciously reaching across to her.

The brown eyes in front of her smiled as she replied back, "Michelle. Thanks for the beer." She lifted it and waved it as a salute. Her confidence seeming to grow. She found herself relaxing and swaying to the music a little, and very much interested in the British bar girl with the crystal blue eyes. They were captivating, and Michelle had trouble looking away.

"New in town?" Cam asked Michelle, wiping up a non-existent spillage on the bar with her cloth as an excuse to linger. She was good with faces usually, and she was ignoring the familiar ones waving bills at her further along the bar.

"Uh, no, not new in town, but uh, yeah new to this I guess." She shrugged, a little embarrassment creeping up to blush her cheeks. It was adorable.

"The bar, or being a lesbian?" Cam chuckled as she tried to gauge whether this beautiful woman was gay or just curious. Enjoying the moment as she took a minute to study her further, she felt a stirring in her core that indicated to her just how much she was enjoying this. Physical attraction to someone had never been a rigid marker for Cam. She was attracted to a lot of different-looking women, and a lot of different things about them could turn her on and create an interest. She didn't really question it generally.

"Both, I suppose." She chuckled too. "I've been thinking about things for some time, but never really—" She paused and thought about it, taking a moment to study Cam, unsure how much of herself to divulge to a complete stranger. "It's difficult."

"Now you can't ignore it any longer?" Cam nodded sagely. She had been there. Pretty much every gay person had had a moment of self-reflection in their life. That moment when fantasy stepped into reality, when acceptance became more than just an acknowledgement.

"Yes, something like that." She spoke honestly and chuckled at herself. She had the cutest laugh, Cam thought to herself. She would have to try and be more comedic in the hope of hearing it again.

Cam excused herself to serve a group of customers, two women who had successfully gained her attention with the bill waving. She couldn't help glancing back at the new woman, who sat quietly watching the scenes play out around her: women, and some men, all enjoying themselves in a place that allowed them to just be.

Locking eyes with each other they both smiled. Cam felt a flutter in her tummy that she hadn't felt in a long, long time, and for just a moment she allowed it to settle, enjoying it and letting it wrap itself around her before she quickly shook it off.

By midnight Cam was due a break. She gave Erin a quick wave and indicated she was leaving the bar. Her eyes swept the dancefloor until she spotted the brunette, moving to the rhythm by herself. She felt a tinge of jealousy as one woman after another attempted to dance with her, silently hoping none of them got lucky. The quiet undertone of attraction was making itself known to her.

Cam sipped on her orange juice, her eyes never leaving the brunette for a second, and when Michelle finally turned and looked back in her direction, it was with a huge smile. Camryn watched as she sauntered back through the crowd of gyrating bodies until she was standing in front of her.

Having gained some Dutch courage, Michelle sidled up beside her and leaned in, her lips almost touching Cam's ear as she inquired, "Can I buy you a drink?" Cam felt her breath against her skin and a shot of electricity seemed to flood her senses in an instance at the closeness. She felt her fingertips begin to tingle, the urgent want in them to reach out and touch and yet, she felt so forbidden and unattainable.

"Sure, why not?" She called over the bar and ordered two more beers while keeping her body in close contact with the brunette in the cap.

Their eyes remained held together, each daring the other to look away first as they took swigs from their bottles. They were roughly the same height, although Cam wore flats and Michelle was in two inch heels. Eventually the tingling fingertips won out when an errant piece of hair gave Cam the opportunity to reach up and tuck it neatly back in place. Her fingers lingered, ghosting gently against the outer shell of an ear. There was a tremor; Cam felt it from them both as her pads slid easily along a strong jawline before dropping back to her side.

"So, I take it you're feeling a little more relaxed now?" Cam asked seriously, her blue eyes squinting as she looked for any sign that she herself was making this woman feel uncomfortable. She wanted everyone who came into OUT to feel at home, to be at ease with the club, the staff and themselves. That was her ultimate dream: to create an environment that was safe for all who needed it, and if she picked up a few hot women along the way, then so be it.

Biting her bottom lip, Michelle nodded shyly. "Yeah, you could say that." Her eyes continued to get lost in the blue in front of her. It was hypnotic.

Cam leant in really close once more and this time, she let her mouth brush Michelle's ear. She saw and felt the reaction it got and asked seductively, "See anyone you like?" Michelle blushed, but her head nodded once more, smiling coyly. She felt elated.

Cam scrutinised her for a moment more. She always knew when a woman wanted her. It wasn't difficult to work out once you learnt to read the signs, and she was getting all the signals from Michelle. She just had to judge if now was the right time to make her move. The last thing she wanted to do was freak her out. But, seeing that Michelle hadn't made any effort to put distance between them since Cam had moved in closer, she inched a little nearer once more, glancing quickly between pools of melted chocolate and plump marshmallow lips. Cam dragged her finger slowly up the arm closest to her and observed as the hairs stood on end, before glancing back up to Michelle's eyes once more, making sure this was all ok. Her chest rose and fell rapidly as her heart rate sped up.

Michelle wasn't dumb; she knew where this was

headed, if she let it. Closer and closer Cam inched forward until she felt soft lips touch her own. She allowed them to stay, met them with her own bravery, timid yet unyielding, they moved unhurriedly against one another until a rhythm built. Camryn smiled into the kiss as it slowly deepened. Michelle followed suit, not quite believing that she was kissing someone – a woman. She felt Cam's finger along her chin, guiding her, keeping her mouth in place with a firm but gentle hold. At some point, she wasn't sure when, Cam felt the eager grasp of fingers against her waist, pulling her closer to the lithe body she wanted to explore with nimble fingers and eager mouth. She could feel Michelle growing ever more courageous, her body responding to the kiss involuntarily, naturally.

When Cam brought her hand up to caress her face and stroke her jawline with her thumb, Michelle in a moment of impulsiveness slid her own palm up and behind Cam's neck, instinctively pulling her in tighter. Michelle moaned and felt herself clenching at the unexpected arousal. Never had she felt anything like this from just a kiss. It was more than a kiss; it was a connection.

The thumping bass that minutes before was all they could hear had become a distant memory of sound. All Cam could hear now was the beating of her own heart as it thumped inside her chest. She enjoyed the instantaneous rush of excitement with the bar side make out session. She hadn't felt like this with anyone in a long time, if at all. However, all too soon the rush of noise crashed back in, filling eardrums with the words of a song she had heard a million times but couldn't for the life of her tell you the name of, as the lack of air caused the kiss to break.

"Wow that was…nice." Michelle groped inwardly, trying to find the right word, but her vocabulary synapses were just not firing. Cam laughed at the notion of that kiss being just 'nice'.

"Nice?! Really? Just nice? I clearly need to do that again if it was just nice!" Cam joked. She really enjoyed making this woman blush and laugh.

"Oh God, no! I mean, it was great!" The flustered brunette tried and failed to backtrack. "Honestly, it was…I didn't plan to do this when I came in here, ya know? I thought I'd just have a few beers and, ya know…kind of just—"

Cam smiled at her. "Its fine. Really, I'm just teasing sweetheart." She laughed some more and then became quite serious, her finger trailing a path along her jaw. In almost a whisper, she said reverently, "God, you are gorgeous!" She leant in, ready to kiss her again. Ready to leave her speechless and wanting, but she didn't get the chance.

A very drunk girl in a tank top and jeans fell against them in her desire to get to Michelle. Cam's drink spilt down her own shirt and all over the floor, but before she had time to react, the girl was lunging for Michelle again.

"Oh my God!" her words slurred, pointing a finger at Michelle. "Shelly Hamlin!! You're Shelly Hamlin," she said loudly. She had clearly had too much to drink as she swayed back and forth, but her face was lit up in some kind of happy place as she tried desperately to focus on the brunette hiding under her cap. From her position, Cam couldn't quite hear what it was that the girl was saying, but it clearly had upset Michelle.

The dark-haired woman stood motionless, instinctively pulling the peak down lower and using her hand to try and cover her face as she shook her head. Noticing the people around them begin to turn and stare at what was going on, Cam instinctively moved closer to shield her.

"No, you're mistaken." She tried to turn away, but the girl kept on reaching out to grab her arm. Cam blocked the move, and then she heard the words. Clear as day.

"It is, you're Shelly! Man, I loved you in *Into the Night*..."

Chapter Five

Cam took one look at the startled woman in front of her, practically frozen to the spot, and suddenly it all fell into place. Shelly Hamlin, actress and star of *Medical Diaries,* was standing right in front of her. The woman she had been kissing just moments ago was Hollywood actress Shelly Hamlin. *Holy shit, how the hell didn't I recognise her?* It was obvious now, as she looked again and paid more attention.

She made a snap decision and grabbed her companion by the elbow, shouting for Gavin across the heads of everyone else. She pointed at the drunk girl and indicated for him to escort her from the premises. She pulled Michelle with her as they moved with ease and speed behind the bar and out through the door marked 'staff only,' not stopping until they were up the stairs and safely ensconced inside her office.

~Out~

Closing the door behind her, she glanced over at Michelle. The woman looked as though she was on the verge of tears or worse. She was shaking, physically trembling; vulnerability came off her in waves, and yet for Camryn it only confirmed her attraction.

"Hey, it's okay." Cam attempted to calm her, impulsively reaching for her, but Michelle shrugged her off as her own arms wrapped around her torso. Cam took a step back, allowing her some space to process.

"Michelle, it's okay, nobody-," she tried again, with words this time, but was cut off instantly.

"Nobody what? Knows that Shelly Hamlin is a raging lesbian!?" She threw her hands up in despair before wrapping her arms tightly around herself again. "I was just kissing you in full view of a bar full of people!" she hissed. "What the hell was I thinking?" The question was clearly rhetorical, and yet Cam felt the urge to answer. She didn't however, knowing silence was probably the best policy right about now.

Michelle, or Shelly, paced the room, back and forth, back and forth, stopping now and then as if she were going to say something before changing her mind and continuing on with her pacing. She grabbed her cap and tossed it angrily across the room while Cam leant back on her palms against the desk and observed her. There wasn't much else she could do.

"I need to get out of here." She glanced toward the door, the only exit. "Shit, shit, shit. I can't—" There was anger building at her own stupidity, fear eclipsing all rational thought as she realised just what she had done.

Unconsciously Cam moved. Without thinking, she placed her palms against Michelle's shoulder and held her at arm's length before finally pulling her into an embrace. She held tight as Michelle struggled to free herself, not from any fear of the blonde, but fear from herself, that she liked it too much. For Camryn, it was instinctive and warranted. She understood the fight or flight reaction, and if Michelle really wanted to, then she could escape her hold on her.

She breathed her in, her scent intoxicating. It was tropical and exotic; mangoes and peach, something spicy.

"It's okay! Nobody else noticed, and she was so drunk she won't remember anything tomorrow and if she does, well she will just assume it was someone that looked like you," Cam told her confidently. "This is Hollywood. There are a lot of beautiful women out there with dark hair. I'm pretty sure when she wakes up in the morning; she isn't going to remember a thing, because she is wasted." She rambled on, trying to find the words that would make it less of a big deal.

The brunette gave up any fight to escape the arms that held her and sobbed against Cam's shoulder. She felt safe in this moment, nestled against this woman she barely knew. She was more confused than she had ever been in her life and yet, all she could think clearly was that she was safe, right here within this embrace.

Gradually the sobbing subsided, but Cam held on to her; she would keep on holding her until she pushed her away. Something innate inside her wouldn't allow her to let go, not just yet.

"It's going to be okay," she reiterated in a whisper to Michelle's ear. The actress looked up slowly, raising her eyes until all she could see was sincerity, nose to nose, breathing in sync.

All at once their lips crushed together once more. Passionate and wanting, these kisses were unlike the one shared before; this time it was frantic. Cam reached up and found the numerous fiddly little buttons on Michelle's shirt while the actress grabbed at the hem of Cams damp top and yanked upwards, breaking their kiss for just seconds until lips collided once more. Fingertips that once ghosted now pressed intently across flesh. Nails scratched lightly against the skin beneath them, pulling and tugging each other ever closer. Belts, buttons and zips were undone, thighs exposed. It was desperate, both women releasing a red hot pent-up tension, extricating themselves from the fears that held each of them back. Reservations and doubts were tossed to one side as they both found something in the other that they needed.

Cam's momentum propelled them backwards until Michelle's lace-covered backside perched on the edge of the desk. With one sweep of her arm, she cleared the counter. Bra clad and breathless, Michelle broke the kiss, giving Camryn the opportunity to take a tour down the neck she had been appreciating all night. Open-mouthed wet kisses trailed all the way down to her shoulder, along her collarbone, before once again sweeping the length of her neck. Cam let her fingertips trail upwards until they encapsulated a soft, lace-covered breast. Her thumb stroked across a taut nipple as the muffled beat of the music from downstairs permeated through the floor and wall, but it was the rhapsody of whimpering, breathing, and fabric rustling that she danced to. She didn't think she had ever been this turned on in her life as she continued her sound exploration of olive skin laid out almost bare in front of her. She wanted to adore it, to take her time and explore every nerve ending that attached to it. What had begun as a frantic ripping off of clothing had now settled to something much more explorative, something more, just *more*. She wanted more. The need to taste her right there on her desk compounded any sense of decency or decorum, and the sounds emitting from Michelle only encouraged her to continue with her mission. She kissed her way down the toned torso, enjoying the way her muscles tensed and relaxed under her touch, and just as her fingers hooked into the waistband of the last boundary to the heaven that awaited her, there was a loud *thump, thump, thump* on the door.

Everything stopped in that instant, both of them frozen in time as panic and fear pushed up the barriers once again and each woman realised what they were doing. There was a surreal feeling about it all; something unexpected had crept up on them both and taken each of them by surprise and yet, neither felt shocked by it.

"Hold on!" Eyes closed, Cam called out to whoever it was that chose right now to disturb them. Opening her eyes to the image of Shelly Hamlin dishevelled, breathing hard in just her underwear, was something she would keep with her, entrenched deep within her memory banks.

Under the scrutiny of Cam's lustful stare, Michelle sat back up grabbing for her clothes. She couldn't help the grin as she hurriedly began pulling them back on, and while Cam did the same with her own clothing, Michelle took the opportunity to enjoy really looking at her long limbs, muscled and strong. For the first time, she acknowledged completely what they had just done, how close she had come to being with a woman for the first time. She didn't regret it; if anything, she was embarrassed for wanting it to continue. She was embarrassed for needing to feel this woman touch her in so many ways and places that she couldn't even fathom how she didn't realise before now exactly what it was she was missing out on. She was turned on and in need of a climax that wasn't going to be forthcoming, not now that the spell had been broken by the loud knocking on the door. Logic and common sense spread through her nervous system, pushing the teasing pleasure out of the way and filling her with fear and panic once again.

She watched as Cam pulled a clean top from her bag and made herself presentable, reaching up and flicking her hair back into its tidy ponytail. It was sweet, the way the blonde turned to her and checked that she was ok with the door being opened. She nodded and readjusted the cap on top of her head and tried to appear nonchalant. Fail.

Erin stood there, a knowing smirk spreading across her features that easily said, 'I am fully aware of what you've been doing in here,' despite that she actually said. "Break's over. I need you downstairs." She looked over Cam's shoulder at the dark-haired woman in the hat and whispered a, "Sorry."

"Okay, I'll be right down." She pushed the door closed slightly before continuing. "Can you tell Gavin I need a word with him? Thank you." Her words were quiet, thoughtful. She wasn't ready for this night to end, but she had a feeling it was about to, so the best she could do was to make sure it ended in the right way.

Closing the door, Cam turned and leant back against it, a million thoughts going through her mind. Looking up, she found Michelle dressed and standing nervously by the edge of the desk, the contents of which lay haphazardly on the floor. She made a mental note that she would need to tidy that up before she left for the night.

Cam smiled warmly. "I'm sorry, it seems as though I am needed back downstairs." The tension still hung in the air between them. Cam considered how she felt and couldn't quite comprehend it. The desire to see this night through was there, of course it was. Michelle, Shelly Hamlin, was beautiful, and this was what Cam did best. One night. But she wanted more; that was the thought that unsettled her. She wanted more than one night.

"Yes! Of course, I—" There was an apprehension to her

voice as it trailed off, looking down at her feet, the confidence of just minutes ago now a memory. She hadn't come here looking for a hook up – well okay, maybe she had always hoped something like this would happen one day, but in reality she hadn't actually come out looking for it tonight and yet here she was, in an office with someone who worked in a bar, someone who knew who she was, and she wasn't fearful of that. No, what scared her was the thought that she might not see her again.

"I wanted to say—" Cam started to walk towards her, but she was interrupted when there was another knock at the door. "Oh, for the love of God!" she muttered under her breath, looking at her with such reverence it made Michelle blush and giggle at the same time.

Cam turned abruptly and reached for the door, yanking it open to find Gavin standing there waiting patiently.

"You wanted to see me?" he asked. He was ex-military and stood virtually to attention whenever he spoke to her. She had tried, in vain, to get him to relax, but after years and years of following orders and being at the beck and call of people he respected, it was near on an impossibility to change his ways now.

"Yes, I need you to make sure my friend gets home safely," she said, as she turned to check with Michelle that it was okay with her. She simply nodded and ambled reluctantly towards the door, but Cam closed it before she could leave.

"Please, two minutes?" she asked of Michelle. She consented with a small nod and Cam quickly opened the door to ask Gavin to wait before closing it abruptly once again.

Moving swiftly, she took Michelle's face in her hands and kissed her mouth; it turned heated the instant their lips met, an immediate heat between them that wasn't going to be doused by simply walking away. Michelle groaned when Cam pulled back, needing to breathe and gather her thoughts. Her eyes ghosted over her face, taking it all in, committing to memory.

"I don't want you to leave," she admitted before fear pushed the next sentence from her lips. "Without my telling you just how much I enjoyed being with you tonight." She said it so sincerely that Michelle thought she must have rehearsed it a thousand times. She tried to leave it at that, but it just wouldn't settle within her. "I really don't want tonight to end but I understand the need for you to go." She reached into her pocket and pulled out a dog-eared business card and put it in Michelle's front trouser pocket, pulling her towards her again for another hot and sensual kiss. "That's my number! If you want to, call me anytime." She breathed deeply. "Of course, I completely understand if you choose not to, and I want to assure you that what happened tonight...it's private."

"Thank you," Michelle said as she kissed Cam's mouth once more, but this time with tenderness and veneration herself. "For everything." And with that, she opened the door and left.

The scent of her still lingered in the air as Cam stood for a moment and inhaled sharply, exhaling slowly. Shaking her head at the absurdity of it all, she laughed at herself for even considering that someone as beautiful and famous as Michelle, Shelly Hamlin, would be interested in her.

Chapter Six

At three a.m., the bar was closed. The staff were busy restocking all the shelves with bottles of beer and juice while the cleaning crew got to work sweeping up the night's filth. It was the only time that Cam felt the loneliness of her life. The noise was gone, the people were gone, and she was left in the office with paperwork and tonight, memories; memories of something amazing. Unlike other times when those memories had just made her grin, this memory caused a different feeling. Frustration. The sight of an almost naked Shelly Hamlin writhing beneath her, the sounds she made when they kissed (and god how she could kiss), had left her bereft of any idea of how to forget about it. She didn't want to.

She grabbed the cash box and went through the bills, counting and filling out her takings sheet before opening the safe and placing everything inside, locking it. Flopping back into her chair, she picked up her mobile phones. She had two, one for work and one that was her private number. There weren't many people who had that number. Opening the screen, she could see a message waiting for her and knew immediately who it was from. Her heart beat a little faster.

Message sent at 1:26 a.m.

"I just wanted to say thank you again for everything, take care M"

Take care; no kiss. The kind of text that reads thanks, but never call me again.

~Out~

By four a.m. the bar was empty. The staff had gone and all that was left to do was to lock up. Throwing her leg over the bike, she sat there and contemplated the night. It had been a rollercoaster of an evening. She was too wired to even think about sleeping. She pulled her helmet on, enjoying the sound of the engine as it purred between her thighs. Taking off down the road like a speedway star, she hoped there were no cops about tonight. She wanted to just yank back the throttle and open up her baby along the coast roads as she wound down from Santa Monica to Redonda beach and back again with thoughts of Michelle, Shelly, Shelly Hamlin accompanying her the entire way.

Not once had Cam sought out famous women to date, and she could do if she so wished. There had been one conquest, Alice, but, like Cam, she had not wanted anything more than the one off on offer. Had she wanted to though, she had the clout to find her way into parties and events that those kinds of women would be at, but the last thing she wanted was to be involved with someone famous. Being followed by paparazzi, having her private life talked about in magazines – no! Fame was not for her and she didn't date, full stop, so why was she even thinking about it?

Because I like her. It was as simple as that; that was the truth of it. There was something about her that had worked its way through her armour and just wouldn't leave. Jesus, of all the times to meet someone that she might have broken the no dating rules for, and she had to be a famous actress hiding in Narnia!

She pulled out her phone, typed a quick message, hitting send before she could talk herself out of it. Then she saved the number to her contacts list. Just in case.

The sun was rising and the sky was changing colours faster than the disco lights at OUT and Cam finally needed to sleep; she was drained, mentally exhausted, and even as she closed her eyes and let her body fall into the comfort of pillows and covers, she couldn't stop herself dreaming of brown eyes and dimples.

Chapter Seven

When Michelle Catherine Hamilton was 9 years old, she already knew that all she would ever want to be was an actress. There was no other option. No back up plan or second choice.

She starred in every school play. She joined every drama club and she signed up for every talent contest there was. Eventually her hard work paid off and at 18 years of age, after a quick name change, she was cast as Tasha Strong. It was a small part in a huge blockbuster, but it had gotten her a lot of attention from all the right people.

Making the biggest decision of her life, she moved lock, stock and barrel from her parents' Midwestern home to the bright lights of Hollywood. It was the best decision she ever made. Within days she was auditioning. She had meetings with agents and eventually signed up with Janice Rashbrook, who was still her agent today.

She added another string to her bow when she was signed by several modelling agencies and found her face and body splashed on every billboard from LA to Kansas. She was an instant household name and from that she went on to land a starring role in one of the biggest cop shows on national TV.

For four seasons she played Andi Stark, a rookie cop with a heart of gold on *Into the Night*. When her character was killed off as the season finale cliff-hanger, there was outrage from the viewing public. So, when she reappeared in her next show, a comedy about three girlfriends competing to date eligible men that travelled through a small town in rural America, she was instantly catapulted to A-list celebrity. However, after several films flunked at the box office, her name dropped off the radar for a few years until she was offered a part in *Medical Diaries*. Originally it was just a three-episode arc guest appearance, but the viewing public once again fell in love with her and she was extended for a longer period; now Shelly Hamlin was one of the lead actors on the show.

Of course, she had always considered she might be a lesbian; she had never shown much interest in boys while she was at school, nor had they played much of a role in her adult life, and she had always found herself passing admiring glances at female models and actresses, putting it down to an interest in fashion or comparing herself. In reality, she now admitted, she was admiring attributes that she found attractive. But, acting would always come first. It was her true love, her real passion. It would always be her dream and would always be the main focus in her life. She couldn't see herself ever settling down with anyone, so she didn't think about it. In her mind, she told herself she would worry about love another day and so, as her career had taken off, she had made do with dating eligible guys. They were good-looking men who were new on the scene or gay themselves and needing eye candy on their arms to go to a movie premier, or just someone to be seen with and talked about at the right time to get some headlines for a new movie or book. A few of them even made it to her bed, but more often than not she ended the night alone. She just wasn't interested in anything that took her focus off her game, at least that was how she told herself it was; in reality she just wasn't attracted to them.

For over 16 years this way of life had served her well, kept her busy. She never felt she was missing out on anything;

that was until she met Jenna.

Jenna James had been her co-star in a play she had taken on over the early summer in New York during the *Medical Diaries* hiatus. Wanting to push her acting skills in a different direction, she took the job based on the fact that Harvey Jacobson was the director. She didn't even read the script. She didn't need to. Just being cast in a Jacobson play was going to give her the challenge she desired.

The play was based on two women who meet in a support group for the bereaved. Jenna played the part of Candice, a bisexual woman coming to terms with losing her son to cancer. Michelle played Nina, a stripper who was having trouble dealing with the loss of her mother. The characters were supposed to help each other to find a happier place.

During rehearsals Jenna made it clear that she understood her character pretty well, being bisexual herself. Michelle was shocked at how open she was about it, but Jenna brushed it off, suggesting that the world was changing. Being bi was actually cool now in many circles, mainly because it wasn't a complete threat to men and their masculinity. They still saw her as a possibility, with the option of a threesome. Plus, she lived in New York, and pretty much everything goes in New York. Over the course of the play's run, they became close, and after one particular night of drinking and laughing, Jenna had kissed her. Michelle pulled away and they never talked about it again, but the experience had given Michelle food for thought. She was turned on.

When she got home to LA, she decided it was time to start exploring her options, but work had resumed and she had to put it on the back burner again until she could resist the urge no longer. That was how she had found herself on the doorstep of OUT. It was considered one of the premier gay bars in WeHo, with many celebrities and high-profile guests spotted enjoying the music and entertainment. Nobody was implying anything about anyone, so as long as she wasn't spotted in the arms of a woman she could just shrug it off to wanting a night dancing. Right?

On her own? In disguise? Who was she kidding? She was going out to see if she liked it, if she could get away with it. Then if she could, she would go back another time and see if she could get lucky with someone in a dark sweaty corner. Maybe.

On reflection, she could now see that the evening had turned out pretty well, and oh boy had she gotten lucky. The blonde was probably the catch of the night; she was sure of it having studied the way other women had tried and failed to flirt with her, but they never seemed to give up. She had even heard a few of them discussing the 'hot Brit' behind the bar and how they couldn't wait to have her hands all over them. So, she was pretty proud of herself to be the one that the blonde chose to hang out with. But, the shock of having that drunken girl recognise her after she had been kissing Cam was something she knew she wasn't ready to deal with. Had anyone else heard or taken notice, she would have been mortified. Thank goodness Cam had had the sense to drag her off to her boss's office. She fully expected Cam to be on the phone to the *National Inquirer* with her insider story scoop, but instead she was shocked to find arms encircling her, strong protective arms drawing her in and comforting her. No power on Earth could have stopped her from kissing the blonde again and god, how wonderful those kisses had been. It was a memory she would not forget in a hurry.

It was still early, a little after 6 a.m., and the sun had just risen as Michelle set off for her morning run. She had barely had any sleep, too wired from the night before to shut out the mental chatter, so many thoughts wrapping around and around her mind that there was no real point in her trying to stay in bed any longer. Not that she ran often, gifted with the luck of not needing to exercise for anything more than the love of it.

She took her usual route and was back within the hour. Still unable to stop thinking about the previous night as she showered, she let her hands touch her own body just as sensually as Cam had done just a few hours earlier. Her fingers deftly sank between her thighs to bring some relief to the constant throbbing. She had never had an experience like it, and she now realised just how much she had wanted to climax under Cam's skilful touch. Not once had she awoken still turned on like this after any other date or sexual encounter. The feeling of warm water as it filtered down her skin re-awoke the imprint of the soft tongue that had mapped her body the previous night. Yes, it had been a quicker experience than she would have liked, but she had never had such a night before, and all she could do was remind herself of it as she came quietly with her back arched against the cold tiles under a torrent of hot water.

Chapter Eight

With a steaming mug of coffee and her phone in hand Michelle found herself sitting on the patio by the pool. The sun was warm already; it was going to be another hot day.

Even on a Sunday, she had to spend her lunch meeting with her agent. After that, she would be free to enjoy the rest of the day. There were some scripts that had come in and her agent was pushing hard for her to look at them. Apparently Gordon Hunter was asking for her personally, so these were exciting times.

Taking a sip of her coffee, she swiped across the glass face of her smart phone. Eight messages already; seriously, did no one sleep in this town anymore? She laughed to herself; well she was up too, wasn't she?

The first three messages were from Janice. Confirming their meeting, changing the time, and then changing the venue. Rolling her eyes, she flicked to the 4th message.

Her heart actually skipped a beat. She wondered how it was possible to feel like a teenager on prom night again, but that was exactly how she did feel: nervous and excited all rolled into one giant ball of confusion.

'You're welcome. I hope you find what you're looking for. Cam x'

Glancing at her watch, she knew it was way too early to call Cam. And what would she say? *'Hi yes, I know we only met last night but I think you might be what I'm looking for?'* How ridiculous would that sound? *'Oh and by the way can we not tell anyone about this, do you mind living your perfect life as a secret to accommodate me in it?"* No, it was best to leave things as they were, wasn't it? This honest, open woman didn't need the hassle a relationship with someone like Shelly Hamlin would bring.

An hour had passed and the other four messages had gone unread as she considered once more whether she should reply to Cam or not. Her heart said yes; her head said no.

If she was really honest then yes, she did want to see Cam again, but she had all these conditions. It just wasn't fair, and could she really trust a woman she met just last night, in a bar, while drinking? The last thing she wanted was to be 'outed.' It had already been too much of a risk. She didn't want to come out, she wasn't ready for that, but she had to admit that she did want more of last night. Was it fair to expect Cam, or anyone for that matter, to accept being a secret to the world? Her life up until now had been so simple, so why would she want to complicate things? Men weren't all bad. She had had some nice, short but nice, relationships in the past. Admittedly none of them had ever turned her on in the same way the girl at the bar had in such a short space of time, but she could live with that, right? She had done ok up till now.

She placed her phone back down on the table and contemplated it some more. The soft scent of flowers wafted in the air as the welcome breeze blew through the garden reminding her of Jenna. Her coffee was now cold, but she didn't mind that so much.

Before she knew it, it was almost 9 a.m. and she needed to get ready for her now brunch meeting with Janice. Pulling on a pair of skinny jeans and a lilac blouse that accentuated her body to its fullest, she felt great. Looking herself up and down in the mirror, she decided she was looking pretty damn good this morning, and it had nothing to do with what she was wearing.

Chapter Nine

Cam awoke to find the sun streaming in through the windows of her beachside residence. She had finally gotten in around 5 am and had literally fallen into bed. The only item of clothing she managed to remove were her boots before sleep made it clear it was not taking no for an answer.

She listened to the squeals of small children running in and out of the surf as they played. The sounds drifting in through the open window reminded her of her own childhood, days in Greece when her parents were still proud of her. She pushed those memories from her mind and reminded herself she was someone to be proud of.

Stretching, she yawned and reached for her phone with one eye half-open. She was disappointed to see Michelle hadn't replied, but the small icon tick showed that she had at least read the message.

The excitement that she had gone to bed with slowly dispersed as she sat up and assessed the situation. Famous movie star, so far in the closet she was virtually in Narnia, clearly she had meant for it to end there. She couldn't deny she was disappointed, which was crazy because she didn't do what her mind kept pushing her to consider. But she knew in her heart, if she was totally honest with herself, she had hoped that by replying to Michelle's original text, it might have led to her being able to steer the conversation so that they could have agreed to meet up for coffee. There didn't have to be any strings to it. She understood the implications of last night and how they had affected the woman she was now daydreaming about. *But technically last night wasn't a date, was it? So you could meet her again, couldn't you?* she thought to herself.

Checking the time on her Rolex, she saw it was almost midday. Hopefully any lingering thoughts of Michelle, Shelly Hamlin, would disappear as the day went on.

~Out~

Wandering barefooted into her kitchen, Cam was greeted by a cheery Maria. The short woman barely reached Cam's shoulders, but Cam wasn't fooled by the diminutive stature of her housekeeper any longer. She could whip a dish towel like a ninja, and Cam had learnt pretty quickly why it was that she always had one tucked into her waistband.

"You look like shit, what time you come home huh?" she demanded to know in her heavily accented English, the word "shit" sounding more like "sheet" to Cam's ears. Maria was one of the people Cam was closest to in life. Officially she was her housekeeper, but they both knew it was more than that. Maria was her glue. She was the woman who made this house a home, the person she could be honest with and expect honesty back, full force 100%, whether she asked for it or not!

"God, I don't even know," she laughed as she grabbed an apple from the bowl. "Anyway, you know I don't need sleep."

Maria took a moment to study her before she turned and poured coffee into two mugs. Placing one in front of Cam she said, "What's her name?"

"Huh? Who?" She sipped the coffee, grimaced, and then poured more milk in before taking another sip. Perfect! She liked her coffee milky, not that Americano rocket fuel that most Americans on TV seemed so hot on.

"The one that's got you all smiley faced today." Maria smiled knowingly at her. She was the mother to two teenage boys; she knew when they were hankering over some girl at school, and it was no different now with this one.

"Why does my good nature have to have anything to do with a woman?" she replied with humour in her voice. She jumped up and sat herself on the countertop, swinging her legs like a kid as she took a bite of the apple.

"I tell you why." Maria poked her arm. "I see you bring girls home and you never have that silly look on your face, that's why."

"Silly look?" she queried, trying to catch her reflection in the glass door to the microwave opposite where she sat. It was true; she did have that look. She didn't need to see a reflection. She could feel it in the tightness of her cheeks, the upturn of her lips and the way in which she felt lighter. Something had lifted, something dark and heavy and cold had moved, shifted from her depths. The thaw had set in.

"Yeah you know, you got this look on your face. Says you're happy, that look isn't there normally," she said. The blonde frowned at her, so she continued. "Oh you smile and laugh and make funny all the time but I see it in your eyes, they don't smile with your mouth. Even when it has plenty to say!" And it was an accurate assessment. Morning after morning, girl after girl, none of them had ever left with Camryn smiling so wildly.

"Can't get anything past you, can I?" Cam said. She jumped down and kissed the top of her matriarch's head. "Her name is Michelle." And with that admission, she strode out of the kitchen, holding her coffee and leaving a smiling Maria shaking her head behind her.

Chapter Ten

Walking into her office later that afternoon, she was instantly transported back to the night before. The smell of the actress's perfume still lingered in the air, and it was intoxicating. She opened the windows and allowed the fresh air to clear the room of any lingering aromas. Hopefully it would clear her mind of any lingering thoughts too.

All she wanted was to get on with the pile of paperwork and not be disturbed, but she wasn't too sure if she would be able to concentrate sitting at the same desk that just hours earlier had had Shelly Hamlin's half naked form writhing on it. She closed her eyes for a moment and sat back in her chair, processing that image once more. It was going to haunt her, she was sure of it.

~Out~

Erin was the first to appear, knocking loudly on the door, just as she had the previous night. She opened it and walked in confidently, more paperwork under her arm and two mugs of coffee in her hands.

"Sorry Cam, but I really need you to sign off on this order for me, oh and also we need to make sure that the DJ is booked for next Saturday, and I think we might have to get some extra staff in for a few shifts," she rattled off before noticing Cam staring off into space. "You ok?" It wasn't often she found her boss sitting in the office just staring at the desk. She passed a mug and the paperwork across the desk to her and sipped her own drink as she waited for an answer.

"Yeah." She shook herself and concentrated on Erin, reaching for the mug with a silent prayer of thanks. "Is that all?" she asked as she signed the order book. "I booked Jose Miguel for next Saturday, it's been confirmed so no need to worry about that."

"Oh right, he was great last time he was here." She took a seat in front of the desk and made herself comfortable, not the least bit ladylike as she planted her feet and leant on her knees with her elbows as she cradled her cup.

"I was thinking about offering him a residency, what do you think?" Cam asked, knowing Erin's opinion would be honest and worth listening to.

"I think that would be a great idea, but he isn't going to be cheap."

"Well, nothing worthwhile is ever going to be cheap, is it?" Cam smirked. "I'll place some ads for staff and then you can take your pick, seeing as they will be your staff."

"What do you mean 'my staff?'" her brow frowned quizzically. She tilted her head slightly and her eyes narrowed as she considered Camryn's words.

"I've been thinking about a few things, and I decided I want to make you the club's manager, officially," she said, looking directly at Erin and noticing her hairstyle had gone from pink to blue overnight. "You've worked for me for almost a year and you already do the job as it is, I can trust you to run this place like it's your own. You'll get a pay rise, of course, but I'll expect you to take on the day to day running of the place. You won't need my signature anymore to place orders, and you can hire your own staff," Cam declared, smiling at her new manager. Erin was silent, mouth agape, and Cam almost wished she had taken a picture. "Of course, if you're not interested..."

"What? No! Wait, of course, really? You're making me manager? Holy shit. What can I say?"

"Thanks? Yes, please, I'll take it?" Cam laughed at Erin, who just sat there looking somewhat bemused. To be fair, she had ambushed her with the idea.

"Yes, of course I'll take it, are you crazy?!" She smiled so wide Cam thought her face might split. "So, a pay raise?" she laughed, rubbing her hands together. This certainly wasn't what she expected to happen this morning when she got to work.

"Get out of here and do some work will ya." Cam snickered and handed back the paperwork that Erin had originally brought in for her to sign. "I'll have a new contract ready by the end of the week."

The door was barely closed when Gavin knocked, eager to speak to her. His usually shy demeanour hid behind a goofy grin as he tapped the door with his knuckles and poked his head around it.

"Hey Boss, just wanted you to know your friend got home safe and sound last night as requested."

"Thank you Gavin, I am most grateful, was she ok?" She ushered him in and indicated the chair that Erin had just vacated, but he didn't take it, instead preferring to stand to attention like always.

"I think so, she was quiet, but she did ask about you. What kind of person you were, that kind of thing," he replied, blushing. He was very cool with Cam being a lesbian, it didn't bother him in the slightest, but he was shy when it came to sex and sexy people. When women hit on him in the club he would literally hide. The girls and boys behind the bar took great pleasure in teasing him just because they thought it was cute.

"Well, I do hope you told her only the good things about me." Cam smiled, actually feeling hopeful at this titbit of information.

"I told her she should find out for herself."

~Out~

The afternoon passed by swiftly, but it hardly felt as if Cam had gotten anything constructive done. Checking the phone periodically on the off chance that Michelle might have texted was futile, and in the end she switched it off completely before she drove herself insane. Tossing it in the drawer and pretending it didn't exist helped immensely. *What is wrong with you? Get a grip.*

She spent an entire hour dealing with her accountant, organising Erin's new pay scale and added benefits. She called up some employment agencies and set up some ads in local newspapers for the extra bar staff, and then she instructed her lawyer to write up a contract of residency to offer Jose Miguel as well a new contract for Erin.

With nothing much left to do and with the clock hitting almost 5 pm, she decided she might as well call it a day. Angie and Fran were bound to be in by now, so she could enjoy a catch up, get a few drinks, and who knew what the night would bring.

~Out~

"Evening ladies, and I do use that term quite loosely." She smiled as both women faked shocked outrage!

"Really Cam, that's how ya treating ya best customers nowadays huh?" Angie deadpanned.

"Customers? That would imply you actually paid for drinks here," she said, just as pokerfaced as she could manage.

All three broke out into laughter and Cam ordered up drinks all round. Sitting down with these two and shooting the breeze was always fun. Fran was a woman of few words, but Angie made up for it with her gentle teasing and bantering. It reminded Cam of home.

"So, are you gonna tell us about Dimples or do we have to get you drunk and drag it out of you?" Angie asked, with an eager Fran nodding by her side.

"Dimples?" Cam laughed, "Nothing to tell," she said with a straight face to two disbelieving ones. "Honestly, nice girl but I don't think she's interested." She shrugged as she picked at the label on the bottle, flicking the tiny pieces of paper across the bar.

"You don't think she's interested?" Fran asked, with an unconvinced raising of her left eyebrow.

"She certainly looked interested when her tongue was down your throat," Angie agreed, laughing at the way Cam tried to dismiss the night before as nothing more than a kiss. They'd both witnessed Camryn in full-on flirt mode. Hell, Angie had even been on the receiving end of it, and they could both see that 'Dimples' was more than interested. Neither woman mentioned that she looked just like that TV star.

"Well clearly my kissing skills are in need of some work!" Cam winked.

"Wanna practise? Fran won't mind, will ya Fran?" Angie winked at Fran and waited for her to agree. They were like yin and yang. One white, one black. One tall, one short. Where Angie was skinny, Fran was curvy. Angie was short haired, Fran had long hair (Though Cam often considered if it was a wig because it changed so often in colour and style), but they clicked and Cam was grateful to have two really good people to call friends.

"That's right, no issue from me." Fran winked back.

"Get lost," she chuckled. "You know the rules."

They all burst out laughing and carried on drinking until Erin appeared, frowning at the sight of the three of them lined up along the end of the bar, beers in hand and grinning like idiots.

"Where is your phone?" she asked, her voice serious as she addressed Camryn.

"It's upstairs in the drawer, why what's up?" She smiled easily at her new manager trying to be serious with her.

"Nothing is up." Erin finally gave in and smirked. "I've had a call from someone with a really sexy voice wanting to know if you were available to speak to her," she continued, watching as the beer bottle in Cam's hand lowered from her mouth slowly, her brain catching up with the information. "I told her you were having a threesome at the bar and to try calling you on your cell, but apparently it's not switched on so, can you call her please at your earliest convenience."

"Clearly the kissing skills are intact then?" Angie yelled exuberantly at Cam's retreating back as the blonde flipped her the finger and stepped behind the bar.

Running up the stairs like an Olympic athlete, she raced to reach the sanctuary of her office and found her phone. She fumbled with the tiny buttons to get it to turn on again; it was taking an age for it to power up. *'Come on, come on'* she whispered impatiently.

Chapter Eleven

Michelle was pacing back and forth across the room. She felt like a teenager, anxious and nervous as she strode back and forth checking her phone every second for the incoming call she hoped would come.

She had been held up almost all day with Janice and hadn't had a second to herself to reply to Cam's message until now. She was worried she had left it too late, but bravery had taken her for a moment and she had made the call. When she realised the phone was switched off, she took it as a sign that she should just give up and went back to worrying once more that Cam had got fed up waiting – or worse still, was with someone else. That thought triggered a jolt of jealousy, an emotion Michelle was not used to having to deal with, and that had prompted her to call again, only this time she made sure that she left a message for the blonde.

The shrill ringing of her phone pulled her from her memory and back into the present. The small screen lit up with 'Cam Calling'. She smiled as she read the screen. The ringing continued on until finally, with one swipe of her finger to the right, she answered the call.

"Hey."

"Hello, how are you? I'm so sorry I missed your call! I left my phone upstairs and I'd switched it off so—" Cam spoke quickly. Her English accent was clear and quite frankly, in Michelle's opinion, sexy as hell!

"That's ok. No harm done, I hope you didn't mind my calling your place of work though?"

"Oh, no it's fine. I can take calls. I'm not actually working right now. I'm glad you called, I didn't think you would." The speed with which she continued to speak silently mortified her.

"To be honest, I didn't think I would either," she chuckled, putting the blonde more at ease and reminding Cam of just how cute she found it when she laughed. "I'm still deciding if this is a good idea."

"Oh, well let's hope you get to a decision quickly then, otherwise this will be a very weird call." Cam laughed, but she realised immediately how disappointed she felt at the honest admission from Michelle. She tried to remind herself that there was nothing in this other than being a friend to someone who needed one.

There was silence for a few seconds, awkwardness seemingly winding its way through both psyches.

"So—" Cam said, pausing but wanting to get straight to the point, "What can I do for you?"

"Well..." Cam heard the hesitation in her voice, but remained quiet so she could say what she wanted to say. "I wondered if maybe you would like to maybe grab something to eat or get a coffee," she asked, nervously.

"Like as in a date or...?" Cam inquired, wanting to make sure she knew exactly what she was getting into. She was cut off immediately.

"Oh, no. I mean, I'm not quite ready for anything like that right now. I...you said, if I needed to talk or—"

"Yes, I would like that," Cam answered quickly before

she could change her mind or Michelle could withdraw the invitation. She had breathed a quick sigh of relief when Michelle had said no; it removed the possibility from the table and Cam could focus on just being a friend. After all, Michelle deserved more than a one night stand for her first venture into the world of lesbian sex.

"Yes?" Michelle exclaimed. This was the most nerve-wracking thing she had done in a long time. To put her trust in this virtual stranger was so unlike her, and yet there was something about the blonde English woman that had immediately left her feeling safe. "So, when – when are you free?" The way she stumbled over her words only endeared her more to Camryn.

"Right now?" Cam suggested hopefully. "Unless that's too soon?"

"Right now?" Michelle repeated, suddenly overcome with more anxieties than she had felt since auditioning for her first ever film part. She hadn't expected that as an answer; she assumed it would be in the week and that she would have several days to back out if she needed to. "Ok, yes, why not?" she found herself agreeing.

"Fantastic! So, where did you want to go? Somewhere discreet?"

"Yes, that would be good."

"Sure, I don't really have a preference, so you pick somewhere you feel comfortable and I will go with that," Cam offered. She knew right away that being subtle about any friendship she had with Michelle would be a top priority. It wouldn't matter that they were only friends if the wrong type of journalist decided to make something of it.

"Thank you."

"What for?"

"For understanding my need for precaution in safeguarding my identity." She winced at how pretentious that just sounded. It was just shy of uttering the infamous 'do you know who I am!' line.

"I've no intention of doing or saying anything that would cause you embarrassment, Michelle." Cam spoke honestly; even if she didn't want to see her again, Cam was not one for kissing and telling.

I hope so. Michelle considered for a moment just how crazy this was, arranging to meet with a woman she had been kissing in public. *Am I asking for trouble?*

"So, I'll see you soon then?" Michelle asked, trying to keep her voice steady. Excitement and nerves fought for dominance.

"Yes. Why don't you text me a time and place while I head home and get changed quickly?"

"Ok, that sounds like a plan."

"Great, then I'll see you later!"

Closing the phone down, Cam gave a little jump and a fist pump. *Oh get a grip Thomas! You are not shagging her so get that right out of your head.*

Grabbing her stuff, she hurried out of the club with

barely a 'see you later' to her friends. Angie, Fran and Erin all gave each other knowing smiles and clinked their bottles together.

"Bout time." Angie smiled as two heads nodded in agreement.

~Out~

As she made her way out of the bar and crossed the small parking lot to her car, the phone beeped, an incoming message from Michelle as requested.

'Hi, looking forward to seeing you. Venice Beach? By the art gallery? 7pm? Michelle x

She felt her tummy flip flop just reading her name. *What the hell was that all about?* It was a strange feeling to suddenly be all sentimental after only a few hours with someone.

Chapter Twelve

Venice beach on a Sunday evening was just as bustling as any other night of the week. People from every walk of life meandered along the boardwalk together. Laughter and chatter mingled with the beat of various musicians who had set up their equipment and began to entertain the passing crowds.

Cafés and restaurants spilled out of their buildings with tables and chairs that lined the outside areas just waiting for customers to fill them. The aroma of food and illegal substances mixed and hung in the air. It was vibrant and noisy and the perfect place to just disappear in amongst the crowd.

Camryn leant leisurely against a graffitied wall. She had chosen to go casual, blue jeans and just a white t-shirt under her black leather jacket. Her hair hung loosely around her face for a change and she had even added a little lip gloss. While she waited, her mind wandered. Since the day she had left Jessica, she had stuck to her guns about women; it hadn't even been a problem for her as most women were content to be just a night of fun. Amanda had been her biggest stumbling block and she had learnt her lesson quickly; it was something she always regretted. But this was different. Yes, she had kissed Michelle, and given the opportunity she would have taken it further, but that hadn't happened and now she was meeting Michelle not as a potential lover, but as a friend. So why did she feel suddenly saddened by that?

Before she could elaborate any further, she noticed the tall figure of Michelle, Shelly Hamlin, sauntering toward her under a big sun hat and sunglasses. *Very Audrey Hepburn.*

White was definitely her colour; her deep tan on olive skin stood out even more. On this occasion it was a white summer dress that flowed almost to the floor, with sandals and a large bag hung over her left arm. Her face lit up, dimples and all, when she spotted Cam through the crowd. She deviated towards her with a small wave of her fingers.

"Hi." A kiss to each cheek. *So very Hollywood.* Cam grinned. "You look great." Cam blushed at the compliment. She was usually the one handing them out.

"Well, I wasn't sure what kind of evening we'd be having with Venice as the venue," she chuckled, looking around them at the eclectic surroundings. "Was there anywhere in particular you wanted to go?"

"No, I have no idea. I'm pretty much winging this whole thing," the actress admitted.

"Ok then, shall we just walk for now and see where it takes us?" The suggestion was as good as any, and they both began to stroll back toward Santa Monica. "I really like it down here, reminds me of Soho back home. It's so.... eclectic!"

"Yes, I don't think I have been there," Michelle replied, her bag now dangling from her hand and swinging between them.

"Oh. Have you not been to London?"

"I have, twice. Both occasions were for work though, so I have never really had the chance to explore. Is that where you're from?" Her inquiry came with a shy smile.

"Uh huh. Born and bred," she smiled sadly. Memories of why she left flooded her mind briefly. Michelle noticed the moment of sadness that passed across her face, but didn't comment on it. "South of the river mind you, the best side."

"Do you miss it?" she asked, her voice soft and gentle despite the gravelly rasp of it. Cam turned her head to face her, and their eyes met and held. For a second she almost told her. In that instant, she was a whisker away from spilling her entire life story, and as she looked into those eyes, she wasn't convinced she wouldn't. A banging drum from one of the bands along the walkway broke the spell and Cam shrugged her shoulders. *What the fuck, I don't even know her and yet she's like a magnet, pulling me towards her.*

"No, not really. I mean I can go back if I want to but—" she looked around and spun on her heels in a circle. "I kinda like it here." Her eyes sparkled under the numerous lights and the fading sunshine.

"It is an amazing place. I couldn't live anywhere else now."

"Not originally from here then?" Cam asked. The need to know everything about her hadn't waned. All morning she had forced herself not to Google her. It had been the hardest thing to do; she wasn't so sure she would be so successful tomorrow.

"Nope, Midwestern girl here. I left a while ago though so, I'm a complete Californian now." They passed a small independent coffee shop, everything organic and Fair Trade. "Do you wanna stop for a coffee?"

"Sure, or we could get takeaway and go sit on the beach." As suggestions went, Cam thought it was a pretty good one; the beach would be quiet and more private for a conversation. *You're not kissing her again!*

Michelle looked down at her dress and considered the option.

"I'll even let you sit on my jacket." Cam smiled.

"Oh so gallant!" she giggled as they pushed their way through the door into the air-conditioned shop.

With paper cups full of hot coffee and a bag of doughnuts in hand, Cam led Michelle across the street towards the beach, her giant hat and sunglasses now placed inside her bag. It was darker the further they walked, the street lights and illumination from the various venues and the pier only a bright back drop.

"So, do you prefer Michelle or Shelly?" Cam asked, her shoes in one hand and a cardboard tray holding both cups in the other.

"Michelle. Shelly is just a part I play, if that makes sense?" she replied. Cam nodded. Michelle carried the donuts, her own shoes also now placed inside her bag. They strolled slowly across the still-warm sand until a lifeguard hut loomed large ahead of them and Cam moved quickly towards it. A single lamp lit the area as though it were a set from a movie.

"I love these! They are *so* iconic! I always think of that dark-haired actress from Baywatch and the red bathing suit as they came running to rescue the idiot that was drowning." She smiled like a kid and Michelle couldn't help but be captivated by her new friend.

"Not Pamela Anderson then?" Michelle asked as she climbed the slope and walked to where Cam now stood, looking over the balustrade. Camryn turned to face her, the lamplight lighting up her features in a way that almost took her breath.

"Nope, I'm a big fan of brunettes." She couldn't stop herself from making the comment and felt her cheeks burn instantly. Michelle smiled but looked away, out to the darkness of the ocean. "Sorry, I didn't mean—"

"No, please it's fine. I just..." She looked intently at Cam as she tried to explain. "Nobody has ever looked at me quite the way you do."

Now it was Camryn's turn to look away. *She has no idea just how beautiful she really is. Get a grip Thomas. She needs a friend, not you perving all over her.* Without another word, she placed the cups of coffee on the deck and shrugged off her jacket. "Shall we?"

"Sure."

They sat together with legs dangling over the side of the deck, each leaning on the frame with a paper cup in hand. The silence was palpable as each woman tried to sort through her own thoughts. Both were conflicted. The attraction was clear, but that wasn't enough. Was it?

Michelle had spoken without truly considering her words. She was being honest; nobody had ever looked at her in the way that Cam did. It was unnerving and yet it made her feel beautiful. She knew she was attractive; she read the headlines and heard people talking about her. She could see it, but she had never really felt it! There had never been anyone who had looked at her so...reverently. Men tended to leer at her and straight women sneered at her, afraid that she would steal their men, but Cam looked at her as though she were the most precious thing she had ever seen.

"I'm sorry, I spoke without thinking...last night—"

"Was really...nice," Cam interrupted. She turned to face her as she smirked, a glint of mischief in her eyes as she used the same adjective Michelle had. She took a huge bite of her doughnut and chewed slowly.

"Yes," she laughed, and bumped her shoulder against Cam's. Her face grew serious once more however when she added, "Really nice, actually." The air around them grew thick, tangible, as if time has suddenly stopped. She watched as the blonde kept her gaze toward the sand, smiling still but unwilling to meet her eyes again. "Should we talk about it?" Now Cam turned to her, her blue eyes boring into Michelle. If she had been standing, she swore she might have felt her legs give way.

"We kissed, it was nice, and now we're hanging out," Cam stated with a shrug, simple and to the point and clearly not what Michelle expected or maybe even wanted to hear.

"Oh, well yes I guess that sums it up." Michelle bit her bottom lip and looked away, feeling more than a little bit stupid. Now it was Cam's turn to watch her companion. She could see the confusion that lingered within her eyes.

"I mean you, you're...you ain't ready for anything else, and me? I don't – I just...I'm not the person you should take things further with. But I can be someone you can trust, talk to, and hang out with. Whatever ya want."

"Why not?" she asked, quietly. She could come up with a

million reasons why someone like Cam wouldn't want to be involved with her, but she wanted to hear the real reason. When she noticed Cam frown, she continued. "Why are you not the person to, to take things further with?" Her cheeks coloured. It was adorable, and Cam wanted to just lean forward and kiss her. *Stop it, stop looking at her like that. Stop looking at her like she is the most beautiful person on the planet. Even if she is.*

Camryn thought for a moment, and that innate need to want to share everything about herself with this woman reared its ugly head again. She pushed it down back into the depths.

"Michelle, I'm just...you're just going to have to trust me on it!" Her coffee was almost gone, but she downed the last dregs anyway.

"It appears I do. I don't know why, but I feel very much at ease with you and I guess...I assumed you felt the same way." She began to wiggle backwards in order to stand, feeling like an idiot. She had been so sure that the previous night had been a prelude to maybe something more, eventually. It was all just so confusing.

Cam scrabbled to her feet and was on them before Michelle, reaching down to help her up. That spark of electricity hurtled through her veins again and hit lower down in a place she desperately didn't want to feel anything right now. It wasn't appropriate!

"I'm sorry," Cam apologised, but she wasn't sure if she was or for what? Being honest or the sparks that flew?

"No, no it's fine. Really, we should be honest, and you're

right. I'm not ready, but I don't believe you when you say you're not the person. I won't ask you to be that person but...I know you could be." She didn't give Cam a chance to reply before she was walking back down the slope and onto the sand, her bag in one hand, heels in the other. Cam watched her for a second before coming to her senses. She tossed their coffee cups into the paper bag and grabbed it along with her jacket and shoes and ran to catch her up.

"Can we...? Will you just...? Wait!" she shouted. "Please just, wait." She stopped running and just stood waiting, watching Michelle as she too came to a halt and waited, the distance between them more than just the physical few feet. She caught up and stepped around the motionless body that stood in front of her. "Look, you...You're the most beautiful woman I think I have ever met and I admit, kissing you it's...there's something...I feel...things but, you...you deserve better. You deserve someone that's...better than me!"

"Why? Because you work in a bar?" She struggled to grasp just why it was such a bad idea. Maybe it was her ego hurting just a little too! She was a movie star, she didn't get turned down.

"No, not because of..." She searched the sky for the words. "Because I will say goodbye the morning after and I...I don't want to say goodbye."

"I don't understand."

"It's complicated. I just met you and I, I like you."

"So, what's the problem?"

Cam was feeling the pressure, what was the problem? "You know what? You just said yourself that you won't ask me to be that person so I don't see that there is a problem."

Michelle listened and nodded and then started to walk again.

"You're right, I gotta go."

Chapter Thirteen

Maria arrived at the beach house the following morning to find her employer and friend passed out on the couch in the living room. Her boots lay haphazardly on the floor, and her jacket was pulled up over her head to block out the light.

"Hey, why you gotta sleep here when I make you a perfectly good bed upstairs?" She spoke loudly as she moved around the room cleaning up the mess from the night before.

"Cos," Cam replied moodily from under the leather blanket.

"Kos is a lettuce, or a Greek island, is not the answer." Maria didn't take any crap off of her and she knew it. The Mexican woman pulled the leather coat from her and folded it neatly.

Cam blinked against the harsh light of day. Stretching out her long limbs, she sat up, looking around the room and remembering how she ended up falling asleep here the night before.

"I got home late, that's all." Which was true. After Michelle walked away and left her alone on the beach, she had started walking. Her mind was in overdrive as she went over and over the conversation and the interactions with the woman who just wouldn't budge from her head.

"Uh huh, where you go?"

"Just walking." Which was also true. She had walked for probably eight or maybe ten miles, she didn't know exactly, but she had ended up in West Hollywood, in a bar.

"Out drinking more like, you stink like a bar." Maria scrunched her nose and stood up. "You should get a shower and then I'll fix you some breakfast."

She strafed her fingers through her hair, wiped her face with her palm hurriedly, and then gingerly stood. Her muscles ached from walking and then dancing. She had had a few drinks, but not as many as Maria assumed. She stank of beer, that was true, but only because the woman she was dancing with had spilt her drink, and most of it had landed on Cam's top. It was becoming a habit!

Walking into her bedroom, she pulled her clothes off and tossed them haphazardly into the laundry basket that sat in the far corner of the room before padding naked into the adjoining shower room. The water was hot and just what she needed to loosen her sore muscles. When she climbed out and wrapped a towel around herself, she noticed the small purplish bruise on her neck and sighed.

Her dance partner had been a little over zealous as they had rubbed up against one another. She had wanted Cam to go home with her, but the blonde just wasn't feeling it. There had been times before when she had turned down the companionship of a lady for the night, but that had always been because Cam had to be up early for work or had an appointment; it was never because she was so hung up on someone else.

When she was dressed and her hair dried enough to tie up, she wandered back downstairs to find what delights Maria had come up with for breakfast. The coffee pot was full and the aroma of freshly ground beans filled the air. She breathed it in and took a seat at the breakfast bar. A plate of French toast was pushed in front of her, with fresh chopped strawberries and kiwi, a bowl of grapes, and a glass of freshly squeezed orange juice accompanied it.

"This is good, thanks Maria," she said, between mouthfuls.

"You're welcome." The housekeeper stood on the opposite side of the bar, palms pressed firmly against the counter, and waited. Cam looked up and caught her gaze. She knew there were two options right now. The hard stare meant she could talk or feel the end of a drying towel as it whipped through the air and slapped against her bare flesh.

"You don't have to look at me like that."

"Like what?" Maria continued her stare, unmoving. Camryn swallowed her mouthful and then took a calming breath.

"You remember I told you all about Jessica? How she hurt me and that from now on I wanted to—"

"You want to pretend you don't feel nothing, yes I remember." Her eyes softened slightly.

"I'm not pretend—there hasn't been anyone since then that I've had any inclination to date." She sipped her coffee and placed the mug back down on the counter, a small clink as porcelain touched marble. Amanda didn't count, even if she had lasted more than one date. Cam had never had any intention of it getting serious.

"Until this Michelle?"

Camryn raised her eyes back up to her mother figure.

"And now you scared," Maria stated.

"It's more complicated than that but yes, it scares me." There was a silence as Maria waited some more. She knew this girl, knew when to push and how hard. "She's...she's famous, Maria, and she isn't out and she's never been with another woman before." She threw her hands up in despair. "I don't even know her, and I have never been more attracted to someone in my entire life," she finally admitted out loud.

"So, it's difficult? You think cos you got all this money that everything is easy now?" She moved around the bar and took a seat next to Camryn, gently tucking her hair behind her ear. "Sometimes, life is hard chica. You can't keep going through it only enjoying the easy things it offers."

"But—"

"There are no buts Camryn, life it don't have time for buts. You like her?" Cam nodded. "Then tell her, take the chance. Give her the chance."

"I don't understand how I can feel like this when I barely know her."

"Sometimes you just have to have faith, something is telling you she is special, right?" Cam nodded. She couldn't argue, even if it made no sense. "You can't let this Jessica keep her grip on your heart. One day you gonna have to share it with someone, God won't give you a choice Camryn."

"And if it goes wrong? If she isn't interested?"

"Then you lost nothing but some pride?"

Camryn couldn't deny that Maria made sense. Whether she understood the whys and wherefores, did it matter?

Cam leant across the space and put her arms around Maria.

"Thank you."

Chapter Fourteen

Monday morning for Michelle had been a late start. She overslept.

She had gotten home early enough after leaving Cam at the beach, but she had sat on her couch with a glass of wine, that swiftly turned into a bottle, and thought things through rather than go to bed. She had no right to be angry with Cam, but she was. She had thought they had a connection and if she was honest, she was hoping that Cam would push her to want more, that if Cam made a move she would have an excuse to say yes, to be brave and take things to another level.

The truth of it was that she was terrified. And now she felt ridiculous too.

~Out~

Michelle's day was going from bad to worse. When she finally arrived at the studio, she found Doug Ramos pacing the lot. A telling-off ensued and she accepted the harsh words that flew her way. Production had been held up for hours by her being delayed and so she took it, got her head down, and worked her ass off for the rest of the day.

When she finally got done around eight p.m., she took the opportunity to unwind in her trailer. She hadn't had a minute to herself all day, and even now, when she finally got around to switching her phone back on, the constant beeping of messages and email notifications coming through hurt her tired brain and she flicked the phone to silent. It was then that she noticed the first message, from Cam.

She felt her heart beat quicken, excitement and apprehension all at once. She tried to imagine what the message could say. She put the phone back down on the side and poured herself a glass of water, sipping slowly while she considered what to do. The answer was simple: she wanted to know what Cam wanted.

"Hi, Can we talk? X"

The message had been sent earlier in the afternoon when Michelle had been shooting scenes. She checked her watch; she didn't know if Cam was working or not so she sent a quick text rather than called.

"Hi, I'm free now."

~Out~

Her phone remained silent the entire journey home. As her car began to near her home, she pressed the button that would activate the electronic gates. They were almost fully open as she pulled in and drove through onto the drive of her palatial Brentwood home.

For five years she had lived here, buying the property from the proceeds of a film she had made several years earlier; it hadn't been the biggest success, but it had paid well. She had then spent the next two years completely renovating it to the modern and stylish property it now was.

She parked her car to the side, but before she could climb out, she noticed movement in the rear-view mirror. A figure appeared, walking in through the gates as they closed up behind her. Thankfully the automatic lighting that came on via the several sensors dotted around the property easily showed the intruder to be tall, blonde, and sexy, all blue jeans and leather jacket again. She composed herself, inhaled deeply, and stepped out of the car.

The chiselled features of the blonde began to smile, a lopsided grin that almost took her breath away. She stood just a few feet in front of her, all her weight on her right leg, her hands tucked into the front pockets of her jeans. There was no denying that Michelle was attracted to everything about her.

"Hey." Cam moved back and forth from one foot to the other. "I got your address from Gavin, I wasn't sure...I didn't want to say what I want to say over the phone. Is this ok?" She looked around, unsure of herself. The cockiness from before was gone. "I can go if—"

"No." Michelle shook her head. "Don't go." She shoved her hand into her bag for her door keys. "Come in, please." She waited for Cam to start moving toward the door before she followed.

Once inside, Cam slipped her shoes off. Her mother had always taught her to remove her shoes when entering anybody else's home; her mother had taught her many things over the years, like how to ignore things, push them deep down and not let them affect you. Her jacket followed and she hung it where Michelle had hung her own before following as Michelle meandered down the hallway. Her eyes automatically fell to the sway of the brunette's hips.

"Would you like a drink? Coffee, something stronger?" the actress asked from the other side of the kitchen island. The house had a completely open feel to it. From where Cam stood at the apex of the kitchen and the lounge, she could also see the dining area and a huge wall of folding doors that led out to what she assumed was a garden. A real fireplace took centre stage against the farthest wall, a giant TV hung solidly along with pieces of art that drew Cam's eye. It reminded her of her own home in many ways.

"Please, whatever you're having will be fine." She was leaning against a wall, hands back in her pockets. Michelle glanced up and noticed her looking toward a piece that she had hanging, a contemporary oil painting of a naked woman. She had never understood until now exactly why she had liked it so much. Now she looked at the profile of Cam and understood innately just how attracted she was to both. She stepped around the island with two glasses, handing one to Cam as she passed her to take a seat on the couch, the same spot she had sat in for hours the previous night.

"So?" Michelle was at a loss as to what else to say, but the silence was more than she could take right now.

"Yeah, sorry," Cam replied. Walking towards the opposite couch, she inquired with a gesture whether she could sit or not. Given the affirmation, she placed her glass on the coaster nearest to her and then took a seat. She sat with her knees together, hands flat against her thighs, rigid and on edge. "I uh…" She exhaled and tried again. "I'm just going to come straight out with it ok? Before I lose my nerve and start running." She tried to smile, but her nerves were winning the battle.

"Ok." Michelle spoke gently.

"So, the thing is. I like you. I haven't stopped thinking about you and you're right, I…I could be that person." Her mouth was dry. She reached for her glass and took a swig of her wine. The cool liquid sliding down her throat was welcome as Michelle tried to concentrate on what she was saying. "And I know...I know that it's difficult for you and that you're not really ready but I wanted you to know that when you are...if you ever get to that place then I...I want-." *Jesus, why was it so hard to say?* "I can't promise that, ya know, it would be easy for me but, if you..."

"Cam? You're right I'm not—" Before she had a chance to finish, Cam was up and moving toward the door. "Cam?" Michelle frowned and followed quickly behind her.

"I – this was...I'm sorry." She found her throat constricting. *Do not cry Thomas, that's not cool!*

"Cam, will you please just listen?" She was now standing right next to her, watching as she was pushing her feet back into her shoes. Michelle did the only thing she knew would get her attention. She kissed her.

Her palms took either side of her face and held firm as she brought her mouth into contact with Cam's lips and pressed hard until Cam stopped trying to escape. When finally the blonde's hands moved and took hold of Michelle's hips, the brunette deepened the kiss, allowing herself to be pressed up against the closest wall. She let her hands wander into hair, grabbing and pulling her closer until all she could think about was the air she needed to breathe.

"I can't promise you that it will be easy for me either," she panted. "Don't go." And then she let go of her hold on her and walked away, back down the hallway to her couch, hoping the blonde would follow and not leave. The wait felt like forever, but then she heard the soft shuffle of shoeless feet as they padded carefully into the room. She smiled up at her and patted the spot next to her. "Let's talk, ok?"

Cam flopped into the chair next to her, her head falling back against the back of the couch, and then turned to look at the actress. Michelle sat facing her, her leg pulled up underneath herself. She was holding her glass of wine and sipping the liquid.

"So, how about I get to tell you how I feel now?"

Cam chuckled and nodded. "I guess that could work." She reached across the table for her own drink and settled back, ready to listen.

"I'm not ready for this," she waved her hand back and forth between them and Cam's heart sank once more, "to become public knowledge. If I entered into any kind of relationship with anyone, then it would have to remain private, secret even."

"Would that be until you're sure? Or forever?" Cam inquired, not that she was bothered too much, but she liked to know the rules. She was good with rules; she knew where she stood and what the boundaries were.

"I can't put a time frame on it. I honestly don't know. Right now I have so much going on that would be jeopardized by any negative press, things that I am tied into with contracts and agreements that I can't get out of."

Cam raised her eyebrow at that. "Why would this," she waved her hand back and forth between them in the same manner that Michelle had just done, "be considered negative?" It always peeved her when the prospect of a same-sex relationship was considered negative, that she was being considered depraved.

"Because, everything I'm paid to do involves the belief that I'm sexually available to men, that the products I'm advertising will improve heterosexual women's opportunities with men, do you see?" The blonde did see. She didn't agree or like it, but she understood what Michelle was telling her.

"If I said that right now, I am happy enough to keep this," Cam again waved her hand back and forth between them, "a secret and that I would never do anything that could jeopardise your privacy, would that be a fair enough answer? On the condition that if this," again with the hand waving, "were this to become serious we could re-evaluate with another conversation down the line?" *Jesus, did I just say that? Serious? Can I really do serious again?*

"Then I would agree that that seems a perfectly reasonable assessment." Michelle reached for Cam's hand and Cam let her take it, interlinking their fingers. "I want to explore this, with you if possible, but I do understand if I am asking for too much from you and—" Cam cut her off.

"I want to explore this too but, I admit it scares me to do so, and I won't make you any promises that I can't keep." Her gaze was so intense that Michelle had a hard time looking anywhere else but those ice blue orbs that just kept drawing her in. She didn't quite know what else to say; she wanted Cam to elaborate, but at the same time this was beginning to sound like a business agreement, and she really wanted romance, not contracts.

"One last question," Michelle said, her eyes locked onto Cam's. "Why does this scare you so much?" She watched that same flash of sadness and even a hint of anger pass across her face as it had the previous evening when they talked about

London.

"Can we just say that things happen in life and I haven't been in the right head space to want that kind of relationship again?"

Michelle nodded.

"I'm not going to lie Michelle, I've been with a lot of women. I just chose not to get involved with any of them. I take them on dates and I – *we* enjoyed our time together and then I say goodbye," she explained, wanting to be honest from the get go. "I'm not a player. I don't search people out in order to hurt them or gain anything from them other than a shared good time without any strings but, I don't invest my emotions in them."

"I see. And that's what you meant when you said I deserved better?"

"Yeah," Cam nodded. "I'm not – I've never met anyone that makes me feel the way you do and that's – it's crazy because I barely know you, I know that but—"

"How do I make you feel?" she asked, her head tilted to lean against the back of the couch, her eyes smiling as she waited for the answer. Cam closed her eyes and inhaled as she considered the question. When she opened them again, she looked at Michelle with complete honesty.

"You make me feel like I can start again. You make me feel like there could be a reason to try something different. You make me feel terrified."

"I get it Cam, I feel the same way. I know I've never been...with a woman before, but I'm not a virgin, when you kiss me? God, I just, everything else fades away and I feel like my insides turn to mush." She chuckled at her own admission and how Cam blushed.

"Oh yeah? From a kiss?" Cam smirked. She put her glass down on the table and moved forward, the cockiness and assuredness back in an instant. "So, if I kiss you now?"

"Just kiss me." She smiled as the blonde neared.

Cam had often read romance novels with lines like, 'they kissed and she saw fireworks go off in her head,' or, 'when their lips touched it lit a fuse of desire that neither could control,' and she had usually skipped past them with a 'Yeah right' muttered under her breath. But as her lips met their match, she couldn't ignore the spark of desire that welled up inside her, the feeling of electricity that tingled through her nervous system and touched every nerve ending with a heat she hadn't ever felt before. She felt alive.

A kiss was usually something Cam did as a prelude to getting naked and enjoying the night, but on this occasion she found she was actually just enjoying the kiss. It was unhurried, gentle pecks and nips that caressed lips. She felt the soft swipe of Michelle's tongue across her bottom lip and smiled at the increased confidence coming from the actress, which in turn gave Michelle what she wanted: access to her mouth. She felt a jolt that rocked her to her core. There was a whimper, and she was pretty sure she was the one who made it. Camryn had never whimpered in her life. Suddenly the room felt like the walls were closing in and she pulled away, panting for breath.

"Jesus!" she exclaimed, her voice barely a whisper as her forehead came to rest against Michelle's.

"You ok?" Michelle asked, smiling as she kissed her lips again, more gently this time.

"Yes, wow!" Cam laughed off her embarrassment. "I'm sorry, I just, wow! Ok, I am officially lost for words."

Michelle laughed. "If it helps, I feel the same way too."

"Yes, it helps!" Cam laughed and kissed her again. "God, I can't get enough, kissing you is like—" She searched her mind for the right word, but it wouldn't come. "I can't describe it but it's a good thing, definitely a good thing." She confirmed with a further kiss.

"I am kind of glad about that." Michelle said, changing her position on the settee so that she could sit against Cam and be held by her.

"Is it crazy that I don't want to take this further?" Cam asked, her mind wandering in directions she hadn't considered for a long time. Michelle's head swivelled to look at her, confusion written all over her face.

"Oh I don't mean-," Cam laughed. "I didn't mean 'this' as in 'us,' I meant as in—" she wanted to explain this properly and not make things worse. "I meant that...ok don't take this the wrong way but usually when I kiss a woman, it's with the intention of taking her clothes off and I...Right now I'm enjoying just being with you, kissing you, and I...I don't feel the need to take your clothes off," she blushed before adding. "Yet."

Michelle breathed out a small sigh of relief. "I think it is crazy, yes, but I like crazy, my life is so hectic at times with people wanting everything from me that actually, I think I like it that you don't want to rush it."

"This would be much more comfortable if I just—" She swung her right leg up, behind and around so Michelle could sit with her back against her chest more comfortably between her legs whilst she herself leant against the arm of the sofa. "There, that is much better." She placed her arms around Michelle's waist. Her chin rested on the brunette's shoulder. "I think I would like to do this again."

"Pretty sure that can be arranged."

Chapter Fifteen

As Cam awoke to daylight streaming in through the large windows, it took a few seconds for her to recall where she was – not that it was the first time that she had woken up somewhere she didn't recognise immediately.

It took another few seconds to understand that she had slept for a second night on a couch. Michelle's couch, along with Michelle, her dark locks spread out across Cam's chest from where she was lying, arm wrapped around the blonde's waist. Camryn tried to move and within moments realised that sleeping on a couch in the same position two nights running wasn't something she wanted to do that often, especially when there were perfectly good beds available. Somehow in the night Michelle had turned and was laying almost face down on top of her. However, when she saw how beautiful Michelle looked as she slept, she decided she was willing to deal with any kind of physical pain sleeping on a couch might create.

"Good morning," Cam croaked at the first sign of movement from the sleepyhead. Her mouth was dry, no doubt from hours of sleeping open-mouthed. She hoped there had been no snoring and was grateful there hadn't been any dribbling. So not the look she was going for.

"Ouch, why do I hurt so—" Michelle said, sitting up and realising the reason. "Oh, I am so sorry, I slept on you all night?" She stifled a giggle, and Cam thought it might just be the most adorable thing she had ever witnessed.

"Strangely, I seem not to mind. Although whether I can actually move to get up is another matter," she laughed, stretching her arms up into the air to work out the kinks in her shoulders.

"What time is it?" Michelle asked. Looking around the room and noting the sunshine that was streaming through the windows, she realised it had to be early still.

"Almost six," Cam replied, looking at her watch. "Do you wanna get some breakfast?" Michelle nodded. "I can't believe I slept on you for 7 hours and you didn't move me?"

"I didn't wake up to notice, and to be fair I don't think I would have." She reached over and stroked her fingers down the side of Michelle's face. "You're very hard to resist." She smiled as she leant in and kissed her good morning properly.

~Out~

"So, what do you have planned for the week?" Michelle asked Cam, grabbing her diary while she sipped her coffee in a local café. They sat opposite each other, distance being the best plan to avoid any spontaneous touching.

Having spent breakfast together, Cam had gone home, needing a change of clothing and a shower as well as having some calls to make. Maria had given her a knowing smirk as she watched her slink up the stairs; the walk of shame she called it whenever Cam came home wearing the same clothes as she had gone out in the night before.

She was barely dressed when her phone had rung. Michelle wanted to meet for dinner after she finished filming, so that was where she found herself: at a table in a small café not too far from Michelle's place well after the sun had set.

"Well, the club is closed till Thursday so I have some time off, but I do have a few things I need to do. I've got some training lined up with my PT later tomorrow, but mainly I'll be lying on the beach and catching up with emails and Facebook, you?"

Flicking back and forth through the pages Michelle replied, "I have a photo-shoot for *MD* tomorrow afternoon, then I'm free. Thursday and Friday I'll be filming again." She looked up, pen between her teeth, and Cam desperately tried not to lean forward and just kiss her.

"So, do you want to maybe spend some more time with me?" She asked the question quietly so as not to be overheard; she was already aware that people around them had noticed Michelle. "Because I know exactly where I want to take you."

"Out?" The little line between Michelle's brows became deeper as she frowned at the possibility of a public date.

"Yes! Well, no, not to the bar!" She giggled at the miscommunication. "But somewhere with me. I promised you we would not do anything or go anywhere that would be risky, but I want us to do what 'normal' people do. Do you trust me?"

"Yes, of course I do." She said the words easily and wondered how it was even possible to be so completely at ease with someone she had just met. "Where do you want to go?"

"Nope, it's a surprise," she teased, tapping the side of her nose with a long finger.

"So, tell me!" Michelle whined in the most appealing way.

"God you are killing me, let's just say it's going to be

epic!" She grinned. "I'm wrapped around your finger already, aren't I?" Cam laughed.

With their meal finished, Michelle insisted on paying, which was fine by Cam as it wasn't a huge bill and with her plans for the following night, she could live with it. They walked slowly, side by side along Sunset until they turned off toward the street that Michelle lived on.

"So, how was work today?" Cam asked. The road that Michelle lived on was quiet, and she dared to walk a little closer to her. Shoulders brushed against each other, but not close enough that anyone watching would make anything of it.

"Better than yesterday. I got into trouble." She stifled laughter at Cam's quizzical face. Being in trouble wasn't something Michelle Hamilton or her alter ego Shelly Hamlin were known for. "Yesterday I was late, I overslept and held up filming for almost two hours. Doug, my boss, was not impressed."

"Oh, why did you oversleep?" Hadn't she left Cam early on Venice? Panic set in as she considered all the other places that Michelle could have gone and who with, which she realised was hypocritical considering she herself went out to a bar and virtually got off with a stranger. She pushed away the jealousy and reminded herself this was new, this was her letting go of the past.

"I spent most of the night with a bottle of wine and the couch trying to work out why I suddenly felt the need to explore...this side of myself and..." She chanced a glance at Cam. In the light of the street lamps she looked pensive, but then she turned and her features relaxed. "I was considering just how it was possible that I had put myself in that position. How we...the kiss." Even in the low light, Cam could see the blush that appeared on her cheeks. "I was thinking how is it possible that someone I just met can turn me on so completely and yet not feel the same way?"

"Ouch." Cam smirked. "You know that's not true."

"I think I am beginning to get that now." She bumped her shoulder against Cam. By the time they finally arrived at Michelle's home, they had discussed the rest of Michelle's day as well as Cam's lazy afternoon at the beach. The mood was easy and light.

"Are you coming in?" Michelle asked as she pushed the key into the lock that held the pedestrian gate to her property closed. They walked through with Cam closing it behind her.

"No, I am going to see you to your door and then I am going to go home and contemplate why I am not currently naked with the most gorgeous woman I have ever met wrapped around me."

Michelle smiled, her dimples deep and enticing.

"I see, but wouldn't you rather cut out that whole 'contemplating' bit and just go straight to the woman wrapped around you part?" Her palms flattened out across Cams shoulders, fingering her lapels she leant in closer. "I don't mind you staying over." Her lips found a place just to the corner of Cam's mouth. "I really don't mind." She punctuated each word with kisses that moved around the edges of Cams lips before finally allowing the blonde to kiss her shamelessly on the doorstep.

"Goodnight." She whispered, backing away with a grin.

Chapter Sixteen

Finishing up her photo shoot, Michelle had plenty of time to get ready for her date with Cam. The bath was hot and full to the brim with deliciously smelling bubbles. The aroma of coconut and mango filled the air as she dipped lower into the warmth of the water and reflected on everything that had happened to her in the last 24 hours, her muscles relaxing as she thought about the possibilities for the night ahead. She was generally a confident person, but she had to be honest with herself that the idea of potentially spending the night with Cam was both exciting and terrifying. She had waited her entire life for this. It was hidden in the depths of her subconscious maybe, but the idea and fantasy had been there all the same, and now she felt mixed emotions. She was virginal in many ways; it was a first time again, but when she considered the way that Cam looked at her, she felt sexy and desired and she desperately wanted to play seductress.

Drying her hair, she decided to wear it up in a ponytail. Having discovered just how much attention Cam had been paying to her neck and just how much she found she enjoyed it, the idea seemed logical as her mind wandered to what else she might find enjoyable.

Sex so far for Michelle Hamilton had not been very satisfying. She realized now that a lot of that was because of her chosen bedfellows; not simply that they were inadequate, but that they were the wrong sex altogether.

She spent thirty minutes going through the racks of clothing she had and finally decided upon a Versace dress.

Assuming that Cam was good to her word and this was going to be a date somewhere discreet, the dress was perfect. It was black like all good first date dresses should be. It was tight and snug in all the right places and gave the illusion that she was wrapped up like a gift just waiting to be ripped open. The cloth wound neatly across her chest and around and down over her left hip before wrapping further around and down to mid-thigh length, leaving her midriff completely bare. The outfit was tempting; it offered a promise of what was to come without being too trashy. But then what else did one expect from Versace! Finishing the outfit with a long black woollen coat, she was ready and on time when the doorbell rang and she pressed the button that would open the gates.

Gavin stood on her doorstep.

"Good evening. Cam asked if I could escort you to the destination. Are you ready to go?" the tall blond asked. Michelle took the opportunity to study him a little. He could have been Cam's brother. They both had the same colouring and height, but where Cam was assured and confident, he appeared a little less so.

"Yes, I am. I'll just grab my bag."

Gavin took the bag from her and opened the door to the Audi so she could get in. Once seated, she considered why it was that Gavin was here and not Cam herself, but she guessed in the grand scheme of things it didn't really matter; she was going on a date.

It wasn't very long before they pulled up at the Marina, an affluent area of LA where yachts and boats of the rich and famous moored alongside one another. They drove slowly along the dockside until eventually he slowed and came to a halt. He got out and opened the door for her before grabbing her bag.

"Thank you," she said. Looking around at her surroundings, she felt confused. They had passed all of the buildings that housed anything that could be construed as a restaurant. There was nothing else out here.

Noticing Michelle's uncertainty, Gavin pointed towards a yacht; not the biggest, but nowhere near being a dinghy. Michelle looked more closely and saw a familiar figure begin to stroll down the gangplank.

"Cam?"

"Hey, come aboard," she shouted down.

Michelle walked confidently towards the yacht and towards Cam. When they reached each other halfway up the gangway, she leant in and kissed Cam's cheek. Gavin followed behind carrying her bag. Once aboard, he slipped past them both and left the bag inside before disembarking with a quick wave.

"Wow, this is beautiful, how did you arrange this?" Michelle asked incredulously as Cam led her onto the deck. She was dressed in navy trousers that fit her like a glove, and Michelle could not stop herself from checking out the tight ass in front of her. She also wore a striped fitted shirt that only enhanced her shape, and a pair of loafers set the entire outfit off. She looked every inch as though she fit right in on board a boat.

"We have our ways." She chuckled and pushed her fingers through her hair as her cheeks blushed a little at the way Michelle was looking at her.

"Ok, I'm not sure how you managed it, but I am impressed." She winked and passed her hand across Cam's cheek, letting her fingers ghost along her jawline to her chin. Smiling, Cam took her by the elbow and guided her inside out of view from anyone who might happen upon them and see them kissing, which was exactly what she planned to do next.

"Would you like some champagne? Or something else?" she asked, having thoroughly greeted her the moment they stepped through the door.

"I would love some champagne, thank you." Michelle grinned. She watched as Cam poured two glasses and brought one over to her.

"So, can I take your coat?"

Smiling, Michelle undid the buttons of her coat and slowly slipped it off, watching with amusement the look on Cam's face as she revealed what could only be described by Cam as the sexiest dress she had ever seen.

"See anyone you like?" Michelle asked coyly, the same question Cam had asked her at the bar on the night they had met, knowing full well what the answer was going to be.

"Oh I'm definitely seeing something. Wow, just...wow."

Michelle blushed profusely as she took in the state of arousal she could see within Cam. Nobody ever looked at her the way that Cam did.

"I feel somewhat underdressed now," Cam declared, indicating her smart pants and shirt. However, not waiting to be invited, she moved right in to kiss her again, deepening the kiss the moment she got the chance. "Jesus, how am I supposed to react when you dress like this?" She blew out a breath as she once more took in the form of the woman standing in front of her. Michelle took a moment to catch her own breath too. Kissing this woman was becoming a habit she now longed to be addicted to. "You look beautiful."

"Maybe I will dress like this every day then if it gets me this kind of reaction," she purred like an expert seductress.

"Oh like you don't get that reaction every day anyway." Cam laughed, but was clearly aroused by the presence of such a glamourous woman standing just feet from her.

As they stood there, eyes locked on one another, there was the sudden rush and roar as the engines started up. Within seconds, a small jolt followed as the yacht began to move away from its mooring.

"Are we moving?" Michelle gasped, her fingers tightening their grip on Cam's shoulder.

"Yes, are you ok with that? I'm sorry, I should have asked you first."

"Yes, it's fine. I just wasn't expecting it; this must be costing a fortune for you to actually take it out to sea?"

Cam had to stifle the giggle that came out; how adorable was this woman? She had no idea about Cam's wealth and that was something else she found very attractive, that for Michelle, money didn't matter; she was just as happy dating someone that she thought worked the bar in a club. However, Cam accepted that by the end of this night she would need to be honest and own up.

"Why are you laughing? That's so mean." The playful slap from Michelle caused them both to laugh.

"Because, you are just so adorable and worrying about my finances when I'm trying to woo you in the most inconspicuous way I can think of."

"Woo me!?" She giggled at the old-fashioned term. "Let me at least pay for things that are needed for my privacy."

"Nope. However, at some point I will call in all debts, but they won't be requiring a cash payment." She winked playfully once more. "And anyway, it's worth every penny." She took a sip of her champagne and enjoyed the light blush that appeared on the cheeks of the woman who was captivating her so easily.

As they got to know one another and caught up on the day, it became increasingly difficult not to kiss. Cam felt the need to touch her, to caress her face or stroke an arm. She snuck quick kisses between words, a smile or a laugh. The entire situation was turning her on, and as the kissing deepened, it took all of her control not to slide her hand up a firm thigh. She lost count of how often she failed to breathe. Kissing Michelle became the only need she had, and air could take a back seat for a while.

Time seemed to fly by, and before either of them knew it, the yacht had come to a stop and the engines cut off. The mechanical sound of the anchor being lowered rumbled through the floor followed by relative silence, just the boat rocking gently as the waves lapped against the hull.

"Please, let me contribute." Michelle tried one last time

to find a fairer way of enjoying these dates. Before Cam could refute her argument once more, they were interrupted by a knock on the internal door.

"You are contributing," Cam insisted. "I just had almost 30 minutes of superior kissing, that has to be worth so much more than fuel for a teeny yacht." She smiled, her eyes lighting up with a sparkle. "Yes?" Cam called out, her eyes finally leaving Michelle's to look towards the door, waiting for whoever had knocked to come in.

"Excuse me, Ms Thomas, but we have arrived at your destination. You are anchored safely for the evening and the crew and I will now depart. If there are any issues, then you know how to contact me. Chef has left instructions in the galley for you as requested." The tall, distinguished man in uniform spoke gently as he explained the situation. Cam stood and sauntered across the room toward him. "I hope you have a wonderful evening, and we will see you again in the morning, when we will be back aboard for 06:00 and have you back on land by the time the sun is up. Good night Miss." Captain John Henderson tilted his head in a slight nod, and Cam shook his hand in thanks.

"Thanks John, I'm sure everything will be fine. Gavin is waiting for you as planned and will take you home and collect you again tomorrow. Oh and John, can you let the boys know how much I appreciate this at such short notice and they will find they have a bonus this week."

"Excellent, I'll pass that message on and will bid you both a good night." The Captain retreated, and a few moments later they heard a small engine being kick started to life on the dinghy that would take the crew back to land.

Cam stood quietly, waiting for Michelle to work it out and ask the questions that, for once, she was going to be happy to answer.

"This is your boat, isn't it?" Michelle asked, finally putting everything together. She nodded slowly as she chewed gently on her bottom lip.

Cam smiled. "Yes it is."

"You own this boat and have a crew on staff?" she said as she stood and began walking slowly, closing the gap between them. Her eyes narrowed as she tried to process how that was possible.

"I do. And I hire them in whenever I need them."

"Including a chef?" she inquired as she reached the spot where Cam stood, hands in pocket, biting her own lip.

"Correct."

"And you work in a bar?" she asked incredulously as her hand reached up and found comfort resting upon the blonde's chest. She drew her fingers down the lapel of her shirt.

"I own the bar," Cam admitted, her voice firm but quiet, not one to shout loudly about her achievements or status.

"You own the bar?" Michelle repeated, nodding her head once more. "Of course you do." She chuckled to herself, her hand making its way up and around Cam, teasing the hair at the base of her neck as her fingers got tangled up with her mane. "Why didn't you tell me?

Cam shrugged. "I dunno, I don't like to talk about things like money. I prefer people to like me for me. But yeah, I own

115

the club and this yacht."

"Is that all?" Michelle teased, her voice barely a whisper as she leaned in and sucked the bottom lip of her date between her own soft lips.

"Are we wanting a list of my assets?" Cam chuckled.

"No. Yes," she laughed. "I thought you worked at the bar!" Her lips moved to the corner of Cam's mouth as another kiss landed.

"I do, I work there all the time."

"So, the office we used the other night wasn't your boss's?" She continued with her questioning as her other hand found a home on Cam's hip, slipping under the striped shirt to touch skin, her thumb rubbing slowly across the flesh.

"No, it's mine," Cam responded with a smile. Her breath hitched as memories flooded straight back into her mind of the night they met. She placed her palms on the hips of the teasing brunette and tugged her closer.

Shaking her head and smiling, Michelle looked intently into her eyes. "You are just full of surprises, aren't you?" she whispered before she kissed Cam's lips once more and placed both of her arms around her neck, bringing them nose to nose.

"I wouldn't ever wish to be considered unimaginative," Cam added. Her nose nudged its counterpart as her lips ghosted over the ones on offer to her.

"Oh, you can trust me that nobody would ever consider you to be unimaginative," Michelle husked, her voice dropping an octave as she flicked her tongue at the cupid's bow on Cam's top lip.

"Fuck," Cam gasped.

"Yes, that's the plan," Michelle whispered before deepening the kiss instinctively. "But not until later." Cam had to steady herself. Who was this woman? She laughed to herself as she realised how much she had underestimated Michelle's own desire.

"So, tell me," Michelle said. "What has Chef left for us?" Cam laughed loudly and took Michelle's hands within her own.

"Shall we go and find out?"

Chapter Seventeen

"Griddled Langoustines with hazelnut butter, followed by pan-fried sea bass with citrus-dressed broccoli and then chocolate and almond puddings with boozy hot chocolate sauce," Cam read from the menu left by her chef, Ricardo, down in the galley.

She bent down and picked up a clean apron. Pulling it over her head, she tied it off behind her back and began reading the instructions. Everything had been prepared and all she needed to do was follow the directions and cook it. Pulling a pan down from the hooks hanging, she stirred the butter in and got the heat going so she could toss in the Langoustines.

"You know it's incredibly arousing watching you cook like this?" Michelle was sitting across the room, one leg crossed over the other, elegantly holding a champagne glass in her hand.

"Really? So, what you're saying is that all I had to do was drag you off to the kitchen and throw some eggs in a pan?

"Well, I'm sure that would have sufficed. However, I think this venue more than holds its own, don't you?"

Cam flipped the giant prawns and began to plate them. "I've never brought anyone here, ya know?" she said, steadfastly following the photograph on how they should look on the plate. "You're the first person." She lifted the plates and carried them to the table. "Other than my friends obviously." She smiled. "But...I've never slept with anyone here."

Michelle thanked her for the food and considered her words. She wasn't telling her about her sex life; it was deeper than that. She was sharing parts of herself that she hadn't shared with anyone else. Michelle was being elevated above all others.

"So you're not mad that I withheld information about myself?" Cam continued, taking her seat next to the actress.

"Nope, in fact now that I know, it makes things between us much easier, doesn't it?" She sliced into the meaty seafood and took a bite. "Oh my god, this is good."

"Yeah?" Cam flushed with pride at the compliment. "So, how is it easier?"

"Well, it's a lot easier to be discreet when it's affordable to both parties," Michelle said.

"That's very true I guess, although I would be quite happy to pay for any opportunity to spend time with you." Cam laughed as she considered what she had just said. "Not that I am in any way calling you a hooker!"

Michelle laughed too. "I could be your Julia Roberts if you like," she whispered, leaning forward to share another kiss.

"I am much better looking than Richard Gere though," Cam smirked. "Maybe not as rich, how rich is he?"

"Oh, you are stunningly better than Richard Gere, and how rich you are doesn't matter. I'd still want to date you if you were a bartender, remember!"

They finished the first course, and while Camryn

cleared the plates, Michelle poured more champagne.

"I love this boat," she exclaimed, a little giddy with the bubbles and the atmosphere.

"Boat? Oh don't let the Captain hear you call it that, it's a yacht. I don't know what the difference is really but they all get very upset if 'she' is called a boat," the blonde teased, tossing a little salt and pepper into the broccoli before tossing it all in the pan. She flipped the fish.

"More champagne?" she offered the brunette, holding a bottle of Veuve Clicquot up in front of her.

"Yes please, should I buy one?" she asked with a wry smile.

"Now why would you need to buy one when there is one already here at your bidding?" The fish was perfect, she hoped! The meal looked exactly like the photograph, so she felt confident as she carried both plates to the table before returning for the bottle of champagne.

"Ah, but it's only available to me while I'm performing sexual favours." She loaded up her fork and held it up for Cam to take a bite.

"And? I see nothing wrong with that arrangement," she laughed. "Mm that is good," she said as the flavours burst inside her mouth.

"You make a good argument," Michelle replied, holding her eye contact.

"You will find I make a lot of good arguments." She really did enjoy this flirty connection they had; a lot of the time

Americans didn't quite understand Cam's humour or comments, but Michelle seemed to just get it, get her.

They finished the meal while they talked. It was all so natural, as if they had been doing this forever. Cam felt so relaxed and comfortable with this woman. Even with Jessica there had always been something that held Cam back. If she was completely honest, she had never felt like this with anyone.

"So," Michelle started, her finger dragging slowly up the nearest arm to her. "I assume we're sleeping here tonight?" She noticed Cam's breathing accelerate and added, "Together?" The blonde nodded, clearly having trouble with her words. Inwardly Michelle giggled at just how easily she could reduce this confident woman to mush. "So, wanna show me where?"

"How about," Cam began, composing herself she leant forward and kissed her forehead, "we finish desert and then I will show you where we will spending our night and you can tell me if it's agreeable." She hoped that Michelle would be on the same page as she was; she wanted to take things slowly, but she also accepted that there was a sexual tension between them that wasn't going to go away anytime soon. It was becoming more difficult to concentrate on everyday things and quite frankly, if she was honest with herself, she didn't want to wait. She was quickly becoming aware that it didn't matter what speed she went; she was falling already, and that was what scared her most. But it was a fear she was willing to finally conquer.

"Ok, but what if the dessert that I want, doesn't come in a bowl?" Michelle's husky voice was low and sexy as she made it clear she was ready to move forward with their relationship.

Cam laughed as she stood. "Come on, grab the glasses, I'll take the bottle."

Chapter Eighteen

Michelle followed her up the steps back towards the deck where they had started from. It was a little confusing; she had assumed any bedroom would be down below, but having never stayed on a yacht before, she guessed it could just be that you had to go up to go down.

Cam lead the gorgeous brunette around the side of the yacht and up toward the front deck, where a large four poster bed sat proudly in the centre.

"Are you fucking kidding me?" Michelle laughed. She raised her hand to her mouth in surprise as she began moving forwards in awe towards the bed, wrapping her hand around a post and swinging around to face Cam.

"I wanted it to be romantic, I thought..." She took a breath and calmed herself. "If we decided to...then I wanted to make love to you under the stars, but we can just sleep if..." Cam whispered, as she wrapped her arms around Michelle's waist.

"And there I was thinking you just wanted to have sex with me," Michelle purred dreamily, wondering if Cam had any idea what it meant to her to have someone want to make love to her like this.

"Oh I do, lots of sex and often! But right now...this minute here under the stars. I wanted to make this unforgettable, something singular and unique...I want to kiss every inch of you and make love with you under the gaze of the universe, in full view of the world around us with no fear of who might judge." She realised she possibly sounded too clichéd, but it was how she felt and right now, she was just going with how she felt.

A solitary tear slid slowly down Michelle's cheek as she listened to the words of someone who wanted her to have the fullest enjoyment life could offer her. Even with the restrictions she had placed on them, Cam had found a way around them; a way to show her off without putting her at risk, and she loved her for it. Not once had any of her previous dates or relationships ever considered her with such reverence. She wiped her cheek and turned slowly in her arms.

"I think I will fall in love with you if you keep this up Cam." She spoke quietly, never once taking her eyes off of her.

~Out~

When Cam brought her hand up to Michelle's face, it was to move a piece of hair that had gotten loose to one side, but as her fingers made contact she felt a surge of something she couldn't quite recognise, but still enjoyed.

"You are so beautiful." They kissed again. It was exhilarating. "Are we really on the same page?"

Michelle nodded, as she turned she threw a glance over her shoulder and commanded, "Unzip me!" Two simple words that made Cam instantly aroused, or was it the look Michelle had given when she had asked the question? It didn't matter.

Cam reached for the hidden zipper and gripped it between two shaking fingertips to slowly drag it downwards, exposing yet more of her spectacular physique. Her skin, there in front of her, just begged to be kissed, and she was happy to oblige. Lips met heated flesh and she kissed her tenderly, dragging her lips delicately down the gap created by the opening zipper. Soft gasps and moans came forth from Michelle as she put her body into Cam's very capable hands.

In just her panties, Michelle climbed onto the bed. She crawled seductively on all fours, all the while watching Cam over her shoulder as she untied the heavy curtains that hung around the sides of the bed frame to allow for privacy should anyone else happen to be sailing by.

With the world outside banished, Cam undressed herself under watchful eyes and climbed up onto the bed with her soon-to-be lover, who had gotten herself more than comfortable against the plump pillows.

Closing the gap between them, Cam brought their bodies together, her hot skin beginning to cool in the night air, but still far from cold. They lay together side by side, face to face as their fingers tentatively reached for one another until arms were wrapped firmly in place.

Michelle giggled nervously and Cam smiled at her. "Are you ok?"

She nodded, assuring her. "More than ok."

Cam needed to kiss her, to ground herself in her. Her fingers moved all by themselves, touching her, caressing her. She needed to feel this, to actually have this connection mean something. Too many times she had refused to allow this to happen. Too often she had given and taken pleasure without giving anything of herself, but this was different. She could feel it in the air, in her heart. *Maria is right,* she thought, *life is too short to not give this a shot.*

"I want you to be that person," Michelle said, reading

her mind as they continued to stare at one another. She wanted this; it was inevitable. It had been a course set in motion from the moment they had first set eyes on each other at the club.

"Are you sure?" Cam asked quietly. Her fingers tenderly touched Michelle's cheek and felt the movement as she nodded.

"Yes." Michelle mirrored the movement from Cam before moving further into her hair – leverage to pull her closer until their mouths met, a ghosting of lips against one another. "I'm not a virgin." She smiled at Cam's hesitance.

"I know." Cam kissed her again, her thumb rubbing gently across her cheekbone. "That doesn't mean I can't...take my time." Her mouth replaced her thumb, tender kisses moving towards her ear. "It's your first time with me," she whispered, enjoying the soft groan that came forth. Her mouth, hot and wet, mapped a trail from ear to collarbone. Whimpers and murmurs sprang forth from Michelle as she relished the attention, attention she had never really had from anyone in a very long time, if ever.

Stopping her ministrations, Cam looked at her, her face deadly serious. "You're shivering?"

"I'm not cold," Michelle answered, her hips rising in anticipation to make contact with her lover.

"If I do something..." Cam continued. She stared into chocolate and melted along with it. "You don't..." She felt Michelle's fingertips travel from their resting place on her hips, up her back and round, her palm flattening out on her chest before sliding up into her hair once more.

"I trust you and I want you." Michelle pulled her down

126

for another kiss. "Please."

Cam smiled, a small nod as she dipped lower. An expletive left Michelle's mouth as Cam's palm joined her mouth and she felt Cam smile knowingly against her breast. She watched as Cam took her time to savour each movement, nearing ever closer to the pebbled nipple that invited her enthusiasm.

Michelle tried to remember if she had ever had this feeling from someone's attention to her body. Her mind was blank; all she could think about right now were the sensations Cam was creating. Her eyes widened as warm lips finally wrapped tenderly around her taut nipple, as fingers travelled and discovered areas of her body she had never paid any mind to.

"Oh God," she whimpered, her own hands holding Cam in place as she pulled her closer, arching her back into her, Cam's fingers beginning to search. There was a trail of fire that followed the fingertips as they explored; she was sure that when it was over she would be covered in red pathways of scorched flesh that would spell out her lover's name, forever burned into her skin. Their hips rocked gently against one another adding more pressure, more and more of her body becoming alive to the touch and feel of her lover's attention. She tried and failed to concentrate on just one thing, but she couldn't. It was impossible; just as she became accustomed to a tongue slowly licking around her nipple, the fingers would move and she would be drawn to them until her centre felt like it would explode with the constant tap, tap, tapping of Cam's heat bumping against her own. She had never felt anything like this.

"Please, I need—"

Cam moved back up her body. Their eyes locked as she searched her face for answers. "Tell me."

Michelle's eyes closed as she concentrated on the continuous tap, tap, tapping of Cam's crotch against her. She could feel herself writhing beneath Cam.

"I...touch me."

Cam smiled at the plea. "Do you trust me?" she asked as she continued to stroke and palm her breast, teasing her beyond anything she had ever known.

"Yes," she inhaled sharply. Her nipple tightened further under Cam's movement as she lingered with every kiss and lick, making her way down through the valley of her chest toward toned abdominals, watching the goose bumps follow in her wake as the sensitive skin caught up with the movement of her hot tongue.

"Everything about you is beautiful," Cam whispered as she kissed the sensitive area of soft skin in the hollows of her hip bones, left then right before sweeping back the entire width just under the edge of her lace panties with her tongue, her intent obvious.

She locked eyes with Michelle, and in that moment she felt everything she needed to. She was consumed with the desire to taste her, worship her, and coax her to climax.

"Ready?" The actress nodded once more, a murmured yes barely audible. She had never been more ready for anything in her life.

Using her fingers, Cam gently tugged at Michelle's panties, peeling them down firm thighs, then calves, then off, leaving her bare and the last remnant of anything physical between them was gone.

Cam placed her hands on her inner thighs and caressed them. Inhaling her scent as she descended, she kept her gaze firmly on the dilated orbs of chocolate that watched her every move. Michelle bucked and squirmed, desperate to have Cam where she needed her the most.

"Fuck," she cried out into the night air when Cam finally took her in her mouth; her body flexed as the blonde took her first taste, her tongue pressed flat, sweeping and swirling. Cam wrapped one arm around her waist, the other reaching for her hand. Fingers clasped together as she took her flying to the edge before backing off and bringing her back again over and over until she lost herself in delirious pleasure and pleaded for release. When it came it was like nothing she had ever experienced before. Her heart thumped and her lungs burned as the breath she held was finally expelled and her body shuddered and trembled as she gripped the sheet with rigid fingers and cried out to the cosmos like a feral animal.

She had had lovers go down on her in the past, but none had ever made her feel like that. Not one had ever stayed there until she was pleasured. It had always been a quick fumble and then on to the main event. But as Cam kissed her way back up her body, she realised just how let down she had been by every previous lover.

"That was…" she breathed heavily, "…amazing." She gasped, smiling and snuggling in further as Cam fell onto her back.

"Yeah?" Cam smiled, her thoughts rapidly swirling around her mind. So many images, sounds and expectations to immerse herself in.

Michelle leant up on her side and regarded her lover as she stared up at the stars. "You ok?"

"I am," she said, nodding and smiling. "I really am."

Michelle laughed and rolled on top of her, supporting herself on her palms she kissed Cam hard. When they parted, their eyes met, but there was a look of nervousness that had settled on Michelle's features.

"What? What is it?" Cam asked, concerned she had done something wrong.

"I just realised something."

"Don't tell me now that you're married with 3 kids and a family dog," Cam teased, trying to laugh it off as she pushed her fingers through the dark locks that framed her lovers face.

"No!" Michelle smiled and then, taking a deep breath, she spoke slowly. "It's just...I've just never done this before. I don't...I'm not sure what to do."

"Oh," Cam said. She had forgotten that little fact in her eagerness to please.

"So, how do you feel about that?" Michelle asked.

"Me? How do I feel? Well, ok." Cam thought for a minute and lifted herself up onto her elbows. Her skin, flushed and sweaty still, was beginning to chill in the night air. "My only concern is that you don't feel pressure to do anything you're not ready or wanting to do, but that would be the case even if you had done this before." She held her lover's gaze. "You don't have to do anything, ok?"

"But I want to," she replied quietly. "I *really* want to, I just...I don't want to get it wrong; I don't want to disappoint you."

Cam smiled, took Michelle's hand in her own, and kissed her knuckles. Gripping her fingers, she said, "You know what these can do." She kissed her mouth. "And you know what this can do." She cupped her cheek, smiling. "And you know where you like to be touched and kissed. So, you just go with it. You can't get this wrong Michelle, don't overthink it. Whatever you do, wherever you touch me, I am going to enjoy it. You know that, right?" She smiled that big smile of hers, eyes that bore deep inside Michelle's soul shining brightly.

Michelle laughed. "Thank you. That has helped!"

"I am glad," she said playfully. "Always here to help."

"Oh you're very helpful," Michelle said, moving to straddle her hips. She leant down, cupping both sides of Cam's face, and kissed her tenderly, her lips playing a smile on her own face.

They giggled and wiggled and slid down the bed together. Cam took Michelle's hand in her own and slowly pulled it to her breast, moving her fingers to show her what she liked. It didn't take much for Michelle's confidence to grow as she began to explore and enjoy touching her lover.

"See, it's easy," Cam grinned, enjoying the attention.

Michelle's fingertips caressed soft skin, exploring. Her

mouth kept busy with those always amazing kisses that allowed her to just sink into the moment and almost forget the nervous anticipation building inside her, to get lost in Cam until the moment she slipped her hand between them and for the first time understood what it was to pleasure another woman. Discovering how aroused Cam was from just kissing and touching her was euphoric. Inciting muffled moans, the writhing body below her pushed her on to further explore and touch and discover all the things that kept this woman stimulated and breathless.

"I need you...inside me," Cam pleaded. The brunette couldn't describe the feeling that built within her when she heard the plea, and she complied; without thinking; without fear. Her fingers reacted just as her body had done when Cam had touched her: instinctively. She felt a surge of excitement as her fingers, in one smooth movement, immersed themselves inside of her lover. Cam almost growled as her hips thrust upward at her touch. Everything revolved around those digits as tentatively they began to follow the rhythm that Cam's hips were setting. But it wasn't enough, not for Michelle. Their eyes met and she smirked at her lover's look of surprise as her mouth lowered to take her first taste, instantly addicted.

"Is that ok?" she questioned. Her confidence had rocketed, but she still had doubts. One night didn't make her a lesbian just yet.

"Yes. So good," Cam gasped, her senses heightened at the new sensation. "Don't stop."

"Oh, I have no intention of stopping." Michelle laughed teasingly as she continued to enjoy the way Cam stretched and hummed until she could hold off no longer and she shattered into a million pieces only to be pulled back together again by the brunette that held her in her arms.

~Out~

Michelle could hardly believe how her body responded to Cam; it was as though she had been given the blueprint to every erogenous zone she had and had memorised them. They had made love several times in the last couple of hours. And it had been making love. Every touch and kiss was filled with a gentleness; it was emotive and beautiful. Yes, it was beautiful. They lay together sated, just enjoying each other.

"Is Cam short for Camilla, Cameron...?" Michelle asked, drawing lazy figures of eight on her lover's stomach with her fingers, amazed at how her abdominal muscles twitched when she glided over a ticklish spot.

"Camryn," she replied, aware since she was a kid that most people would mispronounce her name as Cameron.

"Camryn," Michelle repeated, her voice just a whisper. "I like it."

Cam wrapped her arms around Michelle and snuggled into her. "I'm glad, it would be a real pain to change it." She smiled as she pulled the duvet up over them and kissed the side of Michelle's head. "It's Scottish, my mother's parents were Scots so...I guess it was in honour of them," Cam continued.

"It's nice, suits you."

"It means 'crooked nose,'" she laughed, enjoying the sensations Michelle's fingers were creating on her belly.

"It does not!" Michelle laughed. "Does it?"

Camryn nodded and smiled. "Yep, my parents named me crooked nose."

"Well I think you have a beautiful nose," she laughed as she reached up and drew her finger down its slope.

They both fell quiet, each with thoughts of the other, the dip and rise of the water lulling them into gentle slumber.

The sky was darker now. The moon had moved as the hours had ticked by. The boat rocked gently as Camryn pulled the blankets up and around them. The air was cooler now too, and as she felt her lover relax and begin to fall asleep, she took the opportunity to remind herself that this was all ok. She could do this. Michelle wasn't Jessica.

Chapter Nineteen

It was almost two weeks since their date on the yacht. Eleven days, to be exact, and Cam was finding it difficult to keep herself busy while Michelle was away working.

In the short time they had known each other, Cam had found herself becoming more and more contented with the way their relationship was heading. They hadn't had any conversations with regard to where it would lead, nor had they put any labels on themselves, but from the moment they had met each other, Cam had felt touched by something much more than a fling, and she missed the intimacy of not being physically present with Michelle for such a long period.

They had spent a lot of time talking on the phone, as well as sending text messages and emails almost every hour when possible, but it wasn't the same as being able to actually touch each other. The closeness and tenderness with which they had become so quickly accustomed had become something she now craved. They felt closer though, sharing things with each other they might have otherwise been too shy to say face to face.

With *Medical Diaries* returning to the small screen in the next month, Michelle had got stuck with some last-minute interviews because, although she had filmed all the episodes she was starring in for this season, the cast still had to spend time doing interviews and promos for the upcoming season starter. She was up and down the country with some of the other cast members promoting it before going straight back into filming for the following season. It was non-stop right now.

Cam had managed to catch her several times on morning TV and even caught some of the afternoon chat shows from her office. It was like a cruel gift. On the one hand, she got to see her lover every day; but on the other, she couldn't just reach out and touch her.

She was breathtakingly beautiful, but Cam could tell she was tired. She still answered every question with a smile. She was funny and engaging – the audiences loved her.

Cam, on the other hand, had nothing much to do, so she used this time to do some organizing. She sorted her wardrobe, twice! She had never noticed just how many clothes she had accumulated over the past year or two. Seriously, who needed fourteen white t-shirts?

She spent a few afternoons at the club going through all her paperwork, and that was the dullest thing she had ever done in her life. The only exciting thing to happen was she bought a share in a vineyard in northern Cali and an apartment in Paris.

"Why are you moping around the house and getting under my feet?" Maria asked, as she went about her work that morning.

"Probably because I live here?" Cam replied. With a teasing smile she added, "And I like getting under your feet."

"Well then make yourself useful and fold these towels," she threw back, along with a basket of clean towelling that had just come out of the dryer and was still warm. "So?" Maria said, expecting a reply that would satisfy the question that hadn't actually needed to be verbalised to Cam.

Cam rolled her eyes but answered anyway. "It's nothing, I'm just missing someone I guess, and I'm not used to feeling that way and it's a little unnerving."

"So, why the moping? Is it that Michelle, the one that make you smiley face? Just go take her out."

"I can't." A sad expression complete with pouting bottom lip appeared on Cam's face as she slumped back against the couch.

"You rich. No such thing as can't."

Cam thought about that. Michelle was currently in Dallas. It was 9am in LA, so that meant the time was, what? She grabbed her phone and googled time zones; it was only a two hour difference. And a three and half hour flight. So if she could get a flight, she could be there in just a few hours.

"You are a genius!" Cam exclaimed. She tossed the towels back into the basket and stood, pulling Maria into a huge hug. "I might even give you a bonus."

"Ha you say that every week," Maria shouted after her, the Mexican woman smiling at her pseudo-daughter's retreating form.

~Out~

Arriving at the airport, Cam strolled on up to the desk and purchased a ticket for the next flight to Dallas. She was reminded of that day when she had gone to a different airport and purchased a ticket for the first flight out and ended up here. How her life had taken so many twists and turns, but she was grateful for whatever karma she had earned that had made all this possible.

Her flight was thankfully on time, and she arrived in Dallas at a little after 4pm. It was hot and humid as she stood outside waiting in line for a taxi. She quickly fired off a text to Michelle to find out which hotel she was staying at. When the answer came back with a 'Why?' She smiled but ignored it and replied with. "And which room number?"

By the time she had the answer to both questions, she was already in a cab and headed in her direction. They passed huge glass buildings that towered high into the sky, something she hadn't seen before on such a scale. The sun flashed off of the windows, lighting the way.

~Out~

Michelle had arrived in Dallas late that morning straight from Atlanta, where she and Lisa Marconi, Brad Jensen, and Carl Sterling had done an interview with *Good Morning Atlanta*.

They had arrived straight off the plane and into the studio to record an interview with Kelly and Michael before being driven to the hotel, where they had a free evening to unwind. Then they would be up at 4am to head to the studio for *Good Morning Texas* and onto the next destination: Arizona. It had all become a blur of hotels and studios. It was hectic and she was exhausted. Originally it had been her co-star Selma Quinn who was supposed to be on this trip. However, she had fallen ill, and so they had drafted Shelly in at the last minute. She had had to fly out to New York and then the four of them had criss-crossed the country doing an afternoon show and then a morning show before flying off again.

She was intrigued with Cam when she received a text asking for her hotel details. She expected to receive some flowers any time this afternoon, and the idea made her smile. People sent her flowers all the time, but getting them from Camryn was something she relished as she tried to imagine what kind of flower she would choose. So when there was a knock at the door, she had no hesitation in answering it.

The last thing she expected to find when she opened the door was the tall blonde of her fantasies standing on the other side of it grinning at her. With no time to consider how, when, or why, her face was grasped between two warm palms and her lips were caressed in a bruising kiss as Cam pushed her way into the room and backed her up against the wall, kicking the door closed behind her.

As the kiss broke, Michelle stood dumbfounded and amused when Cam whispered shyly, "I couldn't wait any longer." Before she could comment any further, she was pulled into another searing kiss that left both of them gasping for air. Foreheads touched as their lungs synced together. Inhale and exhale.

"I missed you." Cam said breathlessly as she held her tight against her own body, feeling the calmness wash over her now she finally had eyes on Michelle.

"Yeah?"

"Yeah." She nodded, her nose rubbing up and down its partner before their lips met once more.

"I missed you too Camryn," she whispered back sincerely. In that moment, as they stood there staring at one another, Michelle considered how different her life could be.

"Come on, let me get you a drink." Trying to find some normality, she led her further into the room. The last thing she had expected was to see Camryn today.

"I wasn't sure if you would be happy to see me or not?" Cam said, daring to check out her ass that appeared to be painted into those black trousers she was wearing.

Michelle spun around, confused. She took a moment to really study her and couldn't believe she would think that. "Let me tell you something," she said, walking back towards her. "There hasn't been one day while I have been away that I haven't dreamt of you walking through a door just like that."

"Really?" Cam said, a smile curling on the corner of her lips.

"Really. In fact, I was considering flying home for a few hours when we got to Arizona, just to see you." Flattened palms landed on her lover's chest and pressed lightly as they moved upward.

"You was?" She placed her hands back around Michelle's waist. Her fingers slid effortlessly and unhindered beneath Michelle's blouse.

The feel of Cam's fingertips trailing across her skin felt so natural that she wondered why and how she had ever denied herself this for so long, but then she remembered: it wasn't the act that was causing her to feel this way; it was the woman herself.

"I was," she confirmed, kissing her lightly just to make sure she understood.

"I was worried that my being here might have made you angry," Cam confessed.

"What? Why?" Michelle said, concern evident in her voice. "God, no, never. I would never be angry seeing you."

"I just...you're working and here with colleagues, I wasn't sure if you would appreciate me just turning up but...God it sounds crazy, but I just, I couldn't stay away." Cam admitted. Her finger stroked gently down Michelle's cheek just to emphasise the point.

"Well, had you just arrived downstairs and began shouting for me at the top of your voice, I might have had an issue with it," she joked, wrapping her arms around the blonde's neck. "But I think I can cope with you sneaking into my room." Their lips connected once more and this time Cam lifted her so her legs could wrap around her while she walked her backward, towards the bed.

"How long have we got?" Cam asked.

"Long enough!" Michelle replied as she felt herself being lowered to the bed below them.

Chapter Twenty

Three days later and Michelle found herself on a plane headed back to LA. Selma was well again, and with the upcoming storyline more focused on her character, she was back on the interview trail and Michelle was smiling as the cab dropped her off at home.

"Hey, it's me." She smiled into the handset, imagining Cam sitting in her office. The first thing she had done after dumping her suitcases in the hallway was to call Cam. "Where are you?"

"Hey gorgeous, in my office pretending to do some work." She chuckled, sitting back in her chair and placed her feet up on the desk as she twiddled a pen between her fingers. "You in Memphis yet?" She had a copy of Michelle's schedule on her wall, ostensibly so she could keep up, but in reality it was so she could cross each one off and count the days till she was home.

"Nope." She continued to smile, the phone held in the crook of her neck as she unzipped her skirt and let it fall to the floor of the bathroom. "I didn't make it."

"Oh, you stayed behind in Kansas?" Cam put her feet down on the floor again and leant forward, prepared to leave that very minute and go rescue her if need be.

"No, I came home." She waited for Cam to catch up as she fiddled with the buttons on her blouse, pulling it off and tossing it to the floor too before she pressed the button that would switch on the shower. "I am just going to get in the shower, I should be done by the time you get here."

"On my way, have you eaten? I can pass any and every kind of restaurant. What ya fancy?" Cam's voice was higher pitched as the excitement threaded its way through her being. She was opening and closing drawers looking for her bike keys. She found them in her pocket.

"Other than you? Chinese?" She wandered through to her bedroom and tugged off her underwear, her jewellery following. Naked, she stood in front of the mirror and admired her own reflection. She tried to see herself in the same way that Camryn looked at her. Just the thought of Camryn looking at her aroused her in ways she hadn't known existed.

"Yes, other than me!" Cam chuckled, grabbing her jacket from the back of her chair. "I'll pick something up. See you in a while."

~Out~

On the bike, it took no time at all to collect their food order, and then she was back on the road, feeling rather excited at this unexpected turn of events. When she had gotten back from her trip to Dallas, she had thought it would be at least another week before Michelle would be back, and she had half-heartedly planned to do another spontaneous trip, so this was a bonus she was going to take full advantage of.

When she roared up outside Michelle's she hit the buzzer for the gates to open so she could ride straight in. The gates inched open slowly. As she rode inside the courtyard, she could see Michelle waiting by the door, leaning against the jamb. For a moment Cam had to do a double take. Michelle was wearing a simple blue dress and stood barefooted with her hair still damp and tied up. She was stunning, but she looked almost predatory as she observed her girlfriend.

Kicking out the stand and lifting the helmet off her head before she dismounted, Cam couldn't take her eyes off of her. *God she looks hot.*

"Hey, hungry?" Cam asked, fully intending the double meaning as she grinned. Michelle was like a lioness hunting its prey, her eyes not lifting from Cam. She pushed off from her position against the door and begun walking, no, stalking towards her. As Cam went to swing her leg over the seat she was forcibly stopped in her tracks.

"No, no, no, you do not get to turn up looking like that, riding a bike like that and then just waltz in here without me getting to sample the goods in situ," she growled as she grasped a hold of her leather jacket, pushing her body against Cam as she brought their mouths together. Cam just about managed to hook her helmet onto one of the handlebars before she was engulfed in glorious warmth.

Kissing Camryn Thomas had become something she couldn't live without doing, and if it hadn't have been for Cam's impromptu trip to Dallas, she might have had a real problem to deal with. It was frustrating to know what she was missing and not be able to do anything about it.

"God, you are just way too sexy on this thing." Michelle's tongue slipped easily between welcome lips and made a sound exploration of Cam's mouth.

"Maybe you should go away more often if this is what it's like when you return." Cam smiled into another kiss.

"I can't believe how turned on you make me and you haven't even set foot through the door yet." Her hand flattened out on Cam's chest. Standing forehead to forehead, she closed her eyes and tried to get a grip of herself. She had never been so confident in her ability to show a lover just how aroused she was.

"Well, I tried but I wasn't allowed to get off the bike," she joked softly as she moved her position further to the back of the bike seat, making a space. "Climb aboard!" she offered, taking a good look at the shortness of the dress Michelle was wearing.

Narrowing her eyes at Cam and looking at the dress herself, Michelle laughed. "And just how will that work?"

"Well, thanks to your very secluded garden, all you need to do is this—" She reached out and slowly lifted the dress higher up her thighs to rest at the top of her legs. "Now, swing your right leg over here,"

Holding onto Camryn's shoulder, she swung her leg up and over the seat as instructed, leaving her facing backwards on the bike but opposite Cam, face to face and intimate. A car drove past and a dog barked somewhere in the distance, but all Michelle could hear was the beating of her own heart as she found herself up close and personal with this woman who tantalised and tempted her at every turn.

"Now, if you just rest your legs up here..." Cam made a grab for both of her thighs and slowly pulled her forwards to rest them on top of her own legs, bringing Michelle as close as she could. Her arm slid instantly around her. "Then I can do this!" she declared triumphantly, reaching between them and expertly pushing Michelle's red lace panties to one side, her finger tips brushing softly against her sensitive spot.

"Camryn!" she said in a warning tone, but she made no move to stop her. "What if someone sees us?" she hissed, glancing back and forth before her eyes fluttered closed and her teeth took a hold of her bottom lip. Cam continued to manipulate her, teasing her. "Who can see?" she asked against her ear in a whisper, that voice just as arousing now as it always had been. "Anyway, that's the fun of it."

Swallowing hard but still making no effort to stop the movement of Cam's long, talented fingers, she moaned loudly into the crook of Cam's neck as the blonde moved inside of her without effort or objection.

"Oh God, what are you doing to me?" she asked rhetorically as she raised her head to look Camryn in the eye before she glanced down and surveyed the movement between them.

Cam moved inside her in a slow, torturous exploration. Her other hand slid behind her lover's neck and pulled her in for an equally languid and torturous kiss. The speed of her tongue in Michelle's mouth reflected the speed of her fingers as she urged her to let go and submit to the feelings of pleasure that threatened to course through her nervous system at any minute.

With her impending orgasm building to a climax, Michelle's hold on leather became her only focus. She hid her face in the crook of Cams neck, suffocating her moans and gasps from the outside world, so only Camryn could hear the desire vibrating through her lover's body. When she came, it was with every fibre of her body, her head thrown back in a silent scream before she collapsed against Cam, spent.

~Out~

Dinner was cold. But with the assurance from Cam that Chinese food was always best eaten cold, Michelle plated up the various rice and noodle dishes. She drew the line at cold curry.

"But it's the best part!" Cam said, excitedly. "Seriously, how have you lived this long without trying it?" She grabbed a fork and dug in. She took a huge forkful of chicken dripping in sauce and shoved it right into her mouth and began chewing. "Mm God that is good!"

"Why on Earth would I have tried this before?" Michelle laughed and turned her head away from the offered fork.

"To be fair, I would have assumed an actress in Hollywood lived on lettuce leaves and air before I actually met one and understood, you do eat!" Cam stole another bite from the plastic tray of chicken curry as Michelle pulled a face. "When I was younger, we would go to the pub and get drunk before heading out to a club, then on the way home we would obviously be starving and end up in a Chinese takeaway," Cam explained, picking up the tray and emptying the contents on top of her rice. "And of course, being drunk, you always ordered way too much."

"Of course." Michelle played along; she had absolutely no comprehension because at 18 she was too busy being an actress to be out with friends getting drunk in bars. Not to mention in America you had to be 21 to legally get drunk in a bar!

"You're laughing at me, I know." Cam giggled, pointing

her finger at her. "But I am right... anyhoo."

"Any what?" Michelle roared with laughter. Sometimes when Cam spoke it was like listening to Mary Poppins.

"Anyhoo! Oh come on...ya know, it's a real word!" Cam couldn't help but laugh along with her. She liked being able to make her laugh like this; her laugh had always aroused her right from the start. "*Anyhow!*" she clarified with emphasis. "In the morning, there would be all this cold Chinese in the fridge and we'd all be hung over and starving again and that would be breakfast."

"Oh good grief Camryn, that's disgusting." Michelle picked up her plate. "Can I heat mine in the microwave?" Cam laughed again and grabbed her own plate, saving it from the fate of a microwave murder.

"You can, but...make sure its piping hot otherwise you'll get ill," she said, seriously now. "I really am not very good with vomit," she declared.

"I have no plans to vomit."

"Good, but if ya did then I'd stick around and look after you." Cam smiled shyly. "If ya wanted me to."

"I believe you," she replied, crossing the kitchen to place a sweet kiss against her lips, tasting the curry smudged across them. "Mm, ok that tastes..." She made a grab for Cam's fork and took a mouthful. "Pretty good."

"See, I told ya," Cam said with glee as the actress dived for another bite. "Oh, now you want my food?"

"Yup. Now hand it over," she demanded playfully, and Camryn could do nothing else but obey.

Chapter Twenty–One

The first three days of the week, the bar was usually closed unless for a function or a private hire. Once the bar had been used for a murder scene in a forensic TV show. They had hired the club for three days and even paid all the staff to be extras. It had been fun, but Cam had chosen to stay well behind the camera.

On this particular Tuesday, Cam had asked Michelle to meet her at the club once she was finished with filming. It was going to be quite late, but Cam wasn't concerned. She just wanted to see her and she had the perfect idea in mind for their next date.

She had had to spend most of the weekend at the club dealing with the negotiations over Jose Miguel's contract; finally he had agreed to a 6-month residency, playing every Friday and Saturday night. It was more than Cam had originally hoped for and kept her busy while Michelle had a long-standing weekend away with an old friend, something the two of them did at least once a year and had been planning for months.

When her phone rang just after nine, Cam was upstairs in her office finishing off any last-minute paperwork she had and playing games on her iPad to while away the time. Everything was already set up and ready downstairs.

"Hey baby, you ok?" she asked, seeing Michelle's name appear on the screen. It never failed to make her smile.

"I will be the minute I get out of here and get to you," she sighed.

"I miss you too, so how much longer do I have to wait?" Cam asked as she placed her iPad on the desk in front of her and put her feet up next to it, relaxing into the chair as the sound of the smoky voice pulled her down the phone line. Michelle often commented on Cam's accent, but Cam wasn't sure she knew just how sexy her own voice was.

"We're just finishing up now so I'm hopeful of getting to you within the hour. I just wanted to hear your voice and see if you needed me to bring anything?"

"Nope, I'm all set here babe, just make sure you're wearing something comfortable." Cam smiled into the phone.

"Ok, I can do that," Cam could hear voices in the background and Michelle went quiet as she listened to one of them. "I have to go, but I'll see you soon. I can't wait for you to kiss me again."

"I promise it will be the first thing I do."

And it was. The moment Michelle arrived and Cam saw her, she threw her arms around her and kissed her like her life depended on it.

"I missed you so much," Michelle rasped, clinging to her as they breathed the same air.

"Come on, we have a date to attend to." Cam smiled as she led Michelle into the bar. "Drink?"

"I would love a beer, thank you."

"Beer it is." She sat Michelle down at the bar and wandered around to the other side. Opening a fridge, she grabbed two beers and twisting the caps off, she pushed one across the bar to Michelle, who took a long swig as Cam made her way back around to her. She flicked a switch as she passed; the lights on the dancefloor lit it up and the music kicked in.

"I figured normal people go dancing when they date, so we should do that too." She placed her bottle down on the bar and held her hand out for Michelle to take.

"How do you do this?" Michelle asked incredulously as she took the proffered hand.

"Do what?" Cam was going to play dumb and enjoy the attention.

"How do you make this all so easy? I'm amazed at how you manage to keep finding ways to make us feel like a regular couple."

"We are a regular couple," she replied. "*You* just have an irregular lifestyle." She playfully winked and kissed her cheek. "Dance with me?"

Michelle allowed herself to be pulled toward the dance floor. They spent almost an hour in each other's arms, their bodies rubbing up against each other, hands reaching and grabbing for one another. It was sexy and sensual, and as Michelle turned her back into Cam's front, her arm reached up and around Cam's neck, turning her head slightly so Cam could kiss her mouth as she ground her ass into her lover's crotch. Cam took the opportunity to explore, cupping Michelle's breasts and kneading in time with the beat as their hips gyrated together. She let her hand wander lower, bringing her into contact with Michelle's thighs she inched her dress up, up and up until she could slide her palm across the brunette's flat stomach, inching closer and conquering her underwear.

Teasing her as they moved, it didn't take long for Michelle to feel that familiar feeling brewing deep within her.

"God Camryn, you don't know what you do to me."

"Oh, I think I have some idea." She smirked knowingly as she dipped into the hot well of desire pooling. Cam explored every part of her, teasing to the brink then backing off, all while the beat of the music pumped fluidly around them.

The arm Michelle hung loosely around Cam's neck tightened as she held on. Her other hand gripped at Cam's thigh, nails digging into flesh as she arched and shuddered against her. Michelle had never felt anything like this: being in a public place as she succumbed to her lover's attention. Cam claimed her right there in the middle of the dance floor.

She walked her back to the bar, to the spot they had first met. It hadn't gone unnoticed by Michelle. Turning her, they began to kiss again as Cam lifted her onto the same stool she had first sat on just a few weeks earlier.

"Cam, is this real? I mean, how I am feeling, it's so...overwhelming at times." Michelle spoke with amazement as she stood there with this woman who was slowly becoming the most important person in her life. "It's all just so—"

"I know...I feel it too Michelle." She took her hand and placed it over her heart. "Right here." She was lost in the moment, lost in her eyes as she realised just how much she had fallen for Michelle. There was barely a gap between them but she closed it anyway, allowing her lips to gently press against their counterparts in this combustible sexual tension that seemed to hang in the air whenever they were within sight of each other.

She tugged Michelle's dress upwards again. Groaning inwardly at the sight of Michelle biting her bottom lip in anticipation, she encouraged her to sit on the edge of the stool. "Lift," she instructed in order to drag her ruined underwear slowly down toned legs, tucking them into her pocket for safe keeping.

"Open," she demanded once more, nudging her knees apart. Cam saw the look of intrigue play across her lover's face. "Tell me, what do you want?" She held her gaze and waited.

"You, I want you." It was almost a whisper. "Make me yours." She already knew she was, it was futile to even pretend otherwise; she had belonged to Camryn Thomas the moment she had laid eyes on her.

There were no more barriers between them. Everything Cam had to give she would give her, including this. She held her lover's gaze; recognising the urgent need within her, their eyes remained fixed on one another. Michelle's eyes closed briefly as she felt the gentle touch of her lover as those talented fingers began to explore and invade once more. Brown warmth melted the blue ice as her eyes opened again and settled on the blonde. She focused on the exquisite feeling of her partner moving inside her, every insertion deeper, harder, and faster than the last. Her own hips thrust against talented fingertips, the cadence building.

Everything Cam had to offer, her heart, her soul, it was all there in her eyes as they bore into her, dilated and intent.

She had no idea how long they had been like that, connected together as one, but she could feel the momentum growing, her muscles tensing and tightening as Camryn kept up the rigorous thrust that was propelling her forwards. It was also driving her toward being completely ruined for anyone else, because after this, nobody would ever be good enough for her. Quickly she reached an arm around Camryn's neck, needing to ground herself and stay upright. She clung to anything tangible as she closed up around her lover and held her, gripped tightly within as her body shuddered and shook. Her head rolled back only for Cam to lift it back up.

"Look at me." She smiled, that beautiful smile as those blue eyes came into focus once more.

Their eyes held each other and just as she thought it was over, that she had been given all Cam had to give, she felt it begin again. "I love you," Cam said, barely a whisper as her movement turned gentle and had her lover crying out in a delirious tirade of expletives and pleas to God. She chanted Camryn's name as finally she succumbed again, and this time she didn't need to be told to look at her; it was all she could do to tear her eyes away from this woman whom she needed more than air.

They were as physically and emotionally connected in that moment as two people could be.

Chapter Twenty-Two

Cam's car was parked right out front, the only car in the lot. Today she drove a red Ferrari, a car she had always loved and admired. She had had to wait three months from purchasing it to it being built and ready for her to drive. She had it custom made, insisting on tinted windows and a red leather interior. It sat proudly in a marked space: 'Owner'.

"My place or yours?" Cam asked as they climbed inside the car, the plush leather and immaculate interior impressing itself upon Michelle's senses immediately. She could barely think straight, her mind still lost in the delirium of what they had just shared.

"Yours! I've never been to your place," she noted. "But...I'm not ready to go home yet."

"Ok. Wanna go for a drive first then?" Michelle nodded; a drive would be nice. They could unwind, and then by the time they got back to Cam's place she would be ready to just fall asleep in her arms, or make love. She couldn't wait though to see where Cam lived, and to meet the elusive Maria.

Turning the key in the ignition, Cam pulled the car slowly out of the space and headed for Mulholland Drive with Michelle's palm settled firmly on her thigh. There were plenty of places along that stretch of road to pull into and check out the view and maybe, Cam thought, check out Michelle some more. It didn't seem to matter how often she took her; she just wanted more of her.

The road wound up and through the Hollywood Hills. Michelle rested her palm on Cam's thigh, stroking up and down as they talked and drove. The Ferrari hugged the road with a smoothness that left you wondering if you were even moving, and the night was clear and warm as bugs flew kamikaze at the headlights.

Michelle turned in her seat to face Cam, her palm moving higher with each pass until eventually she reached over and began to undo the button to Cam's jeans. She tugged at the zip until she had it low enough to slide her hand inside.

Cam glanced at her quickly. "What are you doing?" she asked, knowing full well what Michelle was doing. She couldn't help but grin at the image of her actress girlfriend behaving so wantonly.

"I want to touch you, you said I could touch you any time I wanted to and right now...I want to." Her voice was low and suggestive as she dipped her fingers lower until she could feel the evidence of Cam's desire.

"You do realise I'm driving, don't you?" Cam hissed, shifting in her seat to make room while keeping her attention on the road ahead.

Biting her lip, Michelle nodded. "Yes but, I have great faith in your ability to stay in control and keep me... safe," she said, circling her lover's sensitive nub. "As I stroke you and tease you." She pulled her finger out and sucked the wetness off.

"Jesus, 'Chelle do you want me to crash?" she gasped, laughing at her girlfriend's newfound confidence.

"Ya know, I have eaten in some of the best restaurants in the world and I have never tasted anything as exquisite as you," she whispered, her hand dipping back inside Cam's pants once more, only this time they didn't leave. They teased and stroked just like she promised they would.

Driving a car on a winding road in the dark is something of a task for anyone. Having a beautiful movie star's hand down your pants touching you while you're doing it is something else, especially when said beautiful movie star starts talking to you in her wildly seductive voice about all the things she wants to do to you, with you, and for you.

Unable to take much more of it, Cam felt it would be safer to pull in somewhere quiet and just let Michelle, Shelly Hamlin, have her way, because if she didn't then they were in danger of being in an accident. *TV starlet found dead with hand down lesbian lover's pants after horrific car accident* was not a headline Camryn wanted to be a part of.

There were several lookout points along the road, and Cam pulled into the next one she came across. She picked a parking spot as far away as possible from any lighting and switched off the engine. Then she lifted her hips and yanked her trousers down, giving Michelle access all areas.

Laughing, Michelle teased, "Oh, aren't we impatient?"

"Just do it, I can't take much more!" Cam said quite seriously as she fidgeted in her seat.

Michelle knew she had been cruel, but how exciting and erotic it had been to be able to hold this woman a sexual hostage. In all her previous relationships, she had only ever climaxed due to the love making skills of another person a handful of times. Generally, she would have to make an excuse to go to the toilet and finish herself off. Her job, so it had seemed, had been to be the vessel that allowed them to get off, and then they would roll over and fall asleep, assuming they had given her the ride of her life. Yet, here she was with a woman who wanted nothing more than to pleasure her – anytime, anywhere, any way she asked for. Cam never really asked her for anything; she was a woman who gave before she took, and often she gave way more than she ever took. Michelle loved the way she felt these days: content and satisfied beyond her wildest dreams. She wanted to make sure Cam never had to ask for anything from her, that she would instantly know what Cam needed and when she needed it. Right now, Cam needed her.

Unbuckling her seatbelt, she climbed over the centre console and onto Cams lap. It was cramped; the sports car was not built for random sexploits by the roadside. She pushed her hand between them and back into Cams underwear.

"Unzip me," she directed, enjoying the effect those two simple words had on her lover every time she used them.

Cam did as she was told, never once taking her eyes off of Michelle as she shimmied her arms out of her dress

"You like my breasts, don't you?" she inquired knowingly as she pushed her chest forwards toward Cam's eager mouth.

Cam nodded. "Who wouldn't?!" It was true; they were magnificent, and the way they reacted to Cam's touch simply amazed her. She had never had a lover with breasts that were that sensitive.

"I want your mouth on them," Michelle continued, almost reading Cam's mind and becoming more and more confident in her ability to ask for what she wanted.

Camryn nodded again, reaching forward to pull the cup of Michelle's bra down and freeing her nipple from its beautifully constructed constraint.

"God, Cam," Michelle gasped.

Rocking against Michelle's fingers as she sucked the taut nub of sensitive skin between her lips in the confines of the cramped sports car was intense. Michelle began to moan quietly. Listening to the whimpers and groans of her lover as she had her way with her was a huge turn on.

"You like that, baby?" she teased.

"So good, so good, almost there," Cam cried out.

"I wanna hear you come for me." She never realised she enjoyed talking dirty until this very minute, until she had felt Cam's body tighten to her words, her muscles tensed and hard as she peaked. It was erotic; it was public and naughty, and all of that added to the excitement of it.

They kissed and smiled and laughed with each other for a few minutes before noticing a car's headlights slowly making its way towards them.

"Shit. Get dressed," Cam said, hastily redressing as Michelle flopped back into her seat, pulling her dress back on. Cam opened her window and let the fresh air move through the vehicle to remove any trace of sex in the air before she reached over and zipped Michelle back up.

The police car slowed as it passed, the officers taking notice of who was in the car and what they were doing.

Michelle held her breath. The last thing she could afford was to be arrested for indecency. The headlines would be embarrassing, let alone horrific for her career, her family.

"Are you ok?" Cam asked quickly, glancing back and forth between her and the police car.

"I'm not sure, can we get out of here?"

Cam turned the key in the ignition and got the engine running. Reversing out of the parking spot, she turned the car towards the road. Just as they reached the end of the parking lot and were about to make their escape, the familiar whoop of a police siren came from behind them, along with the blues flashing once in the rearview mirror.

"Fuck," Michelle said, quietly. She looked panic-stricken.

"Hey, hey, it's ok. It's going to be fine," Cam assured her. She reached out to touch her hand, but Michelle pulled away quickly. It hurt, but right now she didn't have the time to be concerned about it. So she turned her attention back to the officer as she walked up towards her window. Cam used the electronic button to bring the window back down and squinted as the officer pointed her flashlight at them and got herself prepared to deal with the situation.

"Good evening ma'am," she said, bending lower to take in the car's occupants, her police officer's nose telling her there was something to hide in this vehicle.

"Officer, have we done something wrong?" Cam spoke calmly and directed her gaze to her face, giving the officer her complete attention. Open and honest.

"Not that I'm aware of ma'am. Unfortunately, we get a lot of people parking up here for, shall we say, nefarious motives. Can I ask why you were parked here so late?"

"Oh, just taking in the view. I'm from the UK. I was told the view from up here at night was astonishing and well, it truly is," Cam explained, rambling away quite confidently. The officer was going along with it, but she wasn't born yesterday, and she had seen the movement of two people readjusting themselves too many times. However, on this occasion she hadn't quite been quick enough to catch them in the act, and so there really wasn't anything she could say or do unless she could find another reason to ask more questions. She sniffed the air for drugs, but it was clean of anything like that, so she leant down further to check out the other occupant of the vehicle.

"Ma'am, do I know you?" she asked, her flashlight shining directly at a squinting Shelly Hamlin.

"I don't think we have met, Officer," Michelle replied honestly with a nervous smile.

"Shelly Hamlin? Oh wow, I'm sorry Ma'am, I didn't realise. Well you have a good evening and drive safely now, won't you?" she said, smiling as she realised just what she had stumbled upon.

"Thank you, officer, you have a good night too. Stay safe," Cam said, as she noticed Michelle visibly stiffen at being recognised.

They waited for the officer to get back in her patrol car before steadily driving off. The remainder of the journey was silent. Cam glanced at Michelle a couple of times, but she wouldn't look at her; she just stared out the window, a look of sadness on her face.

As they reached the bottom of Mulholland, she quietly asked Cam to take her home.

When they pulled up outside of Michelle's house in Brentwood, Cam prepared herself for what she knew was coming. Wordlessly, Michelle climbed out of the car and walked away.

She sat outside for a few minutes, waiting for the gates to open for her to drive through or for Michelle to come back out to see why she hadn't followed, but that didn't happen. She needed to compose herself; it was heart breaking to see her lover so frightened and saddened, but there was nothing she could do right now to make it any easier for her, and it was clear she wanted space. She inhaled deeply and reminded herself that tomorrow was another day. Her car reversed back onto the road and she sped off; home was what she needed. She'd have a good night's sleep and then deal with this in the morning once Michelle had had some time to sort through her thoughts.

~Out~

She pulled into the driveway of her beachside home and came to a halt. Reaching into her pocket for her key she found something soft; pulling it free, she looked down and saw a pair of panties. A painful souvenir from a magical moment. She slipped them back into her pocket and let herself in. Pouring a large vodka and tonic, she sat on the beautiful white couch and contemplated how such a wonderful night had gone so wrong.

Chapter Twenty-Three

Fifteen days had passed, slow and torturously long days since that fateful night when everything had changed in an instant, one way and then the other. Cam had honestly believed that once Michelle had had a chance to calm down and scrutinise things in the cold light of *day,* then she would make contact with her and they would just carry on where they left off.

That hadn't happened. She had tried calling, but Michelle never picked up. She sent texts and emails, all of which were ignored. So, she stopped. But she was devastated. She couldn't understand why she wouldn't even talk to her. It hurt. It hurt hard and it hurt deep. At least when things had ended badly with Jessica she had understood why, but this? She couldn't comprehend it.

So she spent more time in the gym, punching things mainly. Bags and pads and anyone brave or stupid enough to climb in the ring with her. It didn't help her to feel any better.

She drank too much, way too much. Vodka had become her friend, her bed mate and companion.

"Hey, why you gotta sleep there and make a mess?" Maria demanded to know when she found her passed out on the couch again.

Cam ignored her and just rolled over. She hadn't slept much in the last few days. Drinking wasn't working, but it didn't stop her from trying to numb the feelings she had welling up inside her. Her own little pity party for one.

"Camryn Thomas what has gotten into you? This is not the way," Maria continued. "You think drinking like this will solve anything?" Maria wasn't blind. Camryn hadn't mentioned Michelle in days, the exact same period of time that she had been drinking like a fish and ignoring anything important. She had had to fend off calls from Erin and Gavin; even her friend Angie had called and Maria had dealt with them all. "She needs time, when she well I send her back to work, till then I deal with her," she told them all. But now, she wasn't so sure she could solve this.

"Don't care," Cam mumbled, and she didn't.

"Well I care and you need to move. I have to clean," she said, poking Cam in the side. "Come on, up, up, up."

"For God's sake. It's all your fault!" Cam shouted as she rolled off the couch and stomped out of the room and straight into her bedroom. She hated the person she was becoming, but it was all she could do not to fall apart completely, and so she withdrew further into herself.

Downstairs Maria shook her head, crossed herself with a muttered quick prayer and then worried.

Chapter Twenty–Four

Sunday night Cam was sick of wallowing in the house and found herself on the dancefloor with a hot brunette. She was drunk and she didn't care who she was dancing with; she just needed someone, anyone, and there had been a lot of offers.

The hot woman was dressed casually in jeans and her shirt was open down to the centre of her chest, allowing just a peek of the promise underneath. She was sexy and fun, and Cam wanted to drown herself in sexy and fun right now.

"Wanna get out of here?" Hot Brunette asked loudly against her ear so as to be heard above the thumping bass music. Cam had been kissing her, they had danced together for most of the night and if she was honest, she missed sex. She hadn't been with anyone since Michelle, but Michelle didn't want her anymore, so what the hell was she waiting for? She would just revert back, back to no strings, no nonsense, and definitely no feelings, sex! Just sex. Good old-fashioned one-night stand sex, and then she would be back to her old self and on the path to getting over Michelle.

"Sure, why not?" Cam smiled in reply. They grabbed a cab. Cam gave the driver the address and then promptly began kissing the brunette again. She was a great kisser. Cam's mind began to wander, but hot and sexy was all over her, bringing her back to the present. Usually Cam was a little more discreet; giving the cab driver a show wasn't her usual style but tonight, she didn't care.

When they got inside Cam's place, she barely had the

door open before Hot Brunette was on her again, touching her and kissing her in all the right places, and she responded to it all. They pulled at each other's clothes and kicked off their shoes as they fumbled their way through the house and up the stairs to the bedroom.

The fact that she was clad in just her underwear and lying on the bed with a woman who wasn't Michelle sliding herself up and down Cam's leg suddenly hit Cam square in the face. The body was amazing but wrong; the face was beautiful but wrong; her scent was nice, but it wasn't Michelle.

"Stop," Cam demanded, as Hot Brunette began a trail down her body.

"Huh?"

"Sorry, I...Can you stop? Please." Cam sat upright, pulling her knees to her chest and wrapping her arms around them. "I can't—"

"What? Are you married or something? Cos I do not cheat with people." Hot Brunette sat up, frustrated. She was virtually naked and as Cam's eyes raked over her face and body, she understood why this woman had ended up in her bed. She was dark haired, olive skinned. Her eyes were chocolate brown and her body shape was...Just like Michelle.

"No, no nothing like that. I just, I can't do this...with you."

"Ok, wanna explain why we're in our underwear on your bed and not fucking right now?" Hot Brunette wrapped her arms around herself too, conscious now of her own nakedness.

Cam got up and quickly pulled a t-shirt and some jogging pants on. She ruffled her hair and thought about everything.

"I thought I – I wanted to but..." She searched for the words she needed and only found the truth. "I'm in love with someone."

"I see, and she isn't around so what, you thought you'd have a quick fling with me?" Anger flashed across the woman's face as she grabbed for the bed sheet.

"No. I don't cheat either, but I feel like I am. I don't even know your name."

"It's Sarah," Sarah said, pulling the sheet up and around her now as she glanced around the room to see where her clothes were.

"Sarah, I am sorry. You're beautiful and fun and sexy, but this is all about me, I love someone else and we broke up and—" Cam tried to explain.

"And you thought you could just have some fun and forget about her, but you can't?" Sarah's voice softened as she began to feel some empathy for the woman she had just been about to ravish.

"Yep, something like that. I'm sorry." She passed the brunette her own top and turned around while she pulled it on. Sarah smiled at the gesture; it was nice, and she felt a small pang of jealousy that this gorgeous woman was so hung up on someone else, someone who clearly didn't know what they were missing out on, or care.

"So, what now?" Sarah asked. "I mean if we're not

fooling around, I should get going?"

"Look, it's 4am, stay and I'll take you home in the morning."

"My car is back at the club."

"Well, then stay and I'll buy you breakfast and then take you back to the club to get your car." Cam tried a half-hearted smile. Sarah really was a beautiful woman, and another time and place who knows, but not now, not this time and place.

"Ok, but I'm warning you I'll be going for the high-end breakfast," she laughed. For the first time since living here, Cam slept in the guest room.

Chapter Twenty–Five

Breakfast was fun, and Cam enjoyed the time she spent with Sarah. It gave her a new perspective about things. As they rode into the car lot at OUT on Cam's bike, she noticed a lot of trucks and people milling around. Monday mornings were usually quiet at the club, unless... *Oh shit.* She had forgotten a film crew were onsite for the day.

She pulled up close to the entrance and held the bike steady as Sarah climbed off. They both removed their helmets, and Sarah leant forward and kissed her. It was a kiss that was more than friendly, enough to say 'you won't forget me' but not enough to say 'I'll see you again'.

"I had fun Cam, maybe you need to start doing that too?" she said, then turned and walked towards her car. Cam watched her, and for the briefest moment she considered going after her. But she knew it wasn't a good idea; it wouldn't be fair to Sarah for a start.

She let out a huge sigh, and as she was getting off the bike she heard Erin shout out to her.

"Great, so you're finally showing up then?" Erin stood with her hands on her hips. She looked much older than her years when she scowled that way. Cam brushed off the attitude.

"Sorry, have I missed something?" Cam inquired, pulling the zipper of her leather jacket down. She knew full well she had and that she really should be apologising instead of riling her friend, but she couldn't stop herself.

"I told you three weeks ago that we have this film crew in, and I told you two days ago that you needed to be here to sign the insurance forms and stuff so they can use the premises for a fire scene."

"Ok, well I'm here now," Cam grouched, "though I don't get why I need to be, this is why I made you manager! To deal with this shit," she complained. Her head was thumping and she needed a drink. Dehydration was kicking in.

"I told you." She was exasperated with her. "As the owner of the building, only you can give permission for them to use it for a fire scene. Otherwise our insurance isn't valid if anything goes wrong!"

"Right." There was a vague recognition of hearing something along those lines at some point in the last few days. She attempted to take a step forward but was stopped in her tracks by a palm against her chest.

"You are not meeting them dressed like that!" Erin looked her up and down in disgust.

"What's wrong with how I am dressed, and who said I am meeting anyone?" Cam retorted, looking down at her leather clad legs. There were a lot of worse ways that she could be dressed.

"Biker leathers, really Cam? Since when has business meant so little to you? And yes, you are meeting them! They have had to delay filming while we waited for you, so you will be Ms Charming this morning." She looked around, thankful that only crew and cast seemed to be in the vicinity to witness this debacle.

"Since I don't have to give a shit, maybe, and no, I am not!" They were getting louder, and heads were beginning to turn and look their way. Erin threw her hands up in the air, frustration mounting.

"Well, I do have to give a shit. You gave me this job to run this club for you, and I am trying to maximise its potential, and I am not having you ruin it because you don't care anymore. Get changed and sign the paperwork and then you can go and not give a shit anywhere you like!" Erin had never spoken to her like that; not once in the entire time they had known each other had Erin even really raised her voice. But instead of it being something that made her stop and think about her own behaviour, it riled her. She was already angry and she needed an outlet. Erin was giving her one and she was going to grasp it with both hands.

"Fine, you don't like what I am wearing? Easily fixed," Cam said, angrily kicking off her boots. She unbuttoned and unzipped her leather trousers. The people working around them had pretty much come to a halt now, too interested in what the two women arguing would do next. She yanked her leather jacket off and tossed it to Erin. "Hold that," she demanded, as Erin stared opened mouthed at what she was seeing.

Cam yanked her leather trousers down and stepped out of them, throwing them at Erin too. She then reached down and grabbing the hem of her T-shirt and pulled that off as well. Now she was standing in just a bra and her skimpy black shorts.

"Any better?" she said, holding her arms out wide and indicating her new attire. Never shy of undressing, Cam was proud of her body and the admiring looks she got whenever

171

she happened to be in the gym or on the beach, and especially in the bedroom, but there were limits and she pretty much just pushed them with Erin.

Erin rolled her eyes, turned, and walked away in complete disgust. Reaching into her bag, Cam pulled out a pair of black combats and a vest top and got dressed. Then she turned and took a sarcastic bow as the men of the film crew applauded and whooped.

"You go girl," One of the most effeminate voices she had ever heard called out, and she almost smiled at the cheeky comment, but as she stood back up and looked to see who had said it, she felt the smirk wiped off her face in an instant as there, standing just feet away and watching her like a hawk, was Michelle.

She was standing next to two other women Cam recognised as actresses on the show, her face impassive. Cam held her gaze as time seemed to stop and nobody else existed. There was a part of her that just wanted to run towards her, to wrap her arms around her and whisper promises that it would all be ok, but she pushed that feeling down and let the ice cloud her eyes once more. She inhaled and blew out a calming breath before turning and walking inside her club and up to her office.

Erin was waiting for her. Cam's jacket had been hung on the hook just inside the door and her pants hung over the back of a chair. She waited for Cam to sit down at her desk before hissing. "Was that really necessary Camryn?"

She thought for a moment. It always reverted back, didn't it, your name. When everyone was happy with you it would be shortened or turned into a nickname, but the minute you stepped out of line it reverted back to its full length. Only her dad ever called her Camryn the entire time. Good or bad, she was always Camryn to him. Her head was all over the place; she had no idea what the hell she was doing anymore and in truth, it scared her a little bit. *And why was Michelle here?*

"Where's the paperwork?" Cam demanded, ignoring the question. *I need to be away from here, anywhere but here.*

"Here!" Erin said. With a sigh, she pointed to a pile of papers on her desk, no longer willing to fight her on this. Cam picked up a pen and scanned through each page, signing where she needed to. Then she placed the pen back down on the desk and stood, ready to leave.

Erin knew today would be hard. When she had taken the booking for *Medical Diaries* to use the space for filming, Cam and Shelly had been an item. She didn't think it would be a problem; in fact, she thought it might have been fun for Cam and Shelly Hamlin. And once she realised it would be a problem, there was nothing she could do; to cancel would be futile for the business and the club's reputation for future location filming. It would be a black mark against them in Hollywood. And it was her job to make this place money and bring it success.

"Anything else? Otherwise, I am out of here," Cam said, leaning on the desk with her palms to steady herself. The sudden urge to vomit began to build as her stomach churned from a mix of last night's alcohol and this morning's shock at seeing Michelle. The room was hot, or maybe it was just Camryn who was feeling the heat.

"No, I don't think so," Erin said softly. She hadn't

realised Michelle would even be here today. She assumed it would be a scene that set up an ER event, but as it happened, some of the cast were going to *be* the ER event, and Michelle's character was involved. "I didn't know she would be here," she said apologetically. Until that moment, Cam hadn't even realised that Erin knew who 'she' was. Erin could see the question on her face, the sudden gulp in her throat as she looked up at her, swallowing down the bile. "I'm not blind, I watch the show. I knew who she was the minute she walked up to the bar." Her boss seemed to consider that for a moment before she spoke next.

"I'm leaving," Cam said quietly, again completely ignoring Erin's comment. To acknowledge it would mean she too had to acknowledge she had just seen Michelle, and she really didn't want to do that; she just wanted to get the hell out of there as quickly as possible and either get drunk or catch a flight.

"Ok, will we see you tonight?"

"No, I'm *leaving*," she emphasised. And to be clear added, "The country."

"What! Why?" Erin shouted, completely unprepared for that. It was one thing to be AWOL for a while until she sorted herself out, but leaving? What about the club and the employees?

"Because I can and because it's what I need to do." Cam spoke quietly, as though admitting it was the hardest thing she had ever done, but she knew that wasn't true; the hardest thing she had to do was to forget all about Michelle, Shelly Hamlin, and she couldn't do that if she stayed here.

"Really? Cam come on, this isn't the way to deal with this," Erin pleaded.

"No? And what is? Because drinking myself to oblivion and neglecting everything I've worked hard for isn't? I can't do this anymore Erin, I need to get away and just clear my head."

"So, you and her? You're over?"

"Seems that way yes," Cam answered as she searched the desk for anything she would need while she was away. She threw a credit card down on the desk. "You can use that for any bills that come up."

"What happened?" Erin followed her lead and ignored what she didn't want or need to discuss right now.

"Honestly? I fell in love and then...I don't know." And she didn't. At first she put it down to fear, waiting to read a headline that suggested something about the police stop, but there wasn't anything, and she had bought every tabloid magazine and paper for a week just to be sure.

"It makes no sense," Erin said, as if reading Cam's mind. She had seen them together that night, seen how happy Cam had been these past few weeks, and now she was a shell of that person. She knew Cam was right; getting away from here was probably for the best. "What shall I tell anyone that asks?"

"I'm out of the country. I don't care. You are in charge here. I'll call when I have the details and check in while I'm away, but I'll have my phone with me."

"When are you leaving?"

"As soon as I make arrangements with Steven, he is

pretty good at organising me a jet when I need one. So, tomorrow probably."

"And this is really what you want?" she asked.

"Look at me. I look like how I feel. I don't sleep, I'm drinking too much, I need to do this before I – I need to fix this." Cam's eyes spoke a thousand words that Erin didn't need to hear to understand.

"You can't just get out there and find a woman to fuck and be done with it?" Erin asked.

Cam gave Erin a sad smile. "Tried that last night, couldn't do it. I'm leaving my bike here. I'll take the car home and then get a cab to the airport tomorrow," she said, tossing the bike keys into her desk drawer and picking up the keys for the Ferrari.

She walked out of the room and Erin listened as her usually chipper boss slumped down the steps one by one. She usually flew up and down them with a spring in her step. Erin threw her pen down on the table and whistled. *Someone finally got through that armour and planted a damn bomb, that's for sure.*

~Out~

Cam exited the club and headed straight for her car, not looking up or around. The last thing she wanted to do was see Michelle again. So she moved quickly and efficiently towards her vehicle. As she blipped the alarm key fob, the small group of guys hanging around it all turned to see who was going to be driving the sleek red car. They made a few comments about the vehicle and a couple even threw a joke or two in about the impromptu strip show they had witnessed. She threw a hard glare their way but otherwise ignored them as she climbed in. Once the engine was engaged, she wasted no time and accelerated out of the parking lot as quickly as she could. She didn't see Michelle watching her leave. She didn't see the tears that flowed.

Chapter Twenty–Six

Michelle had spent the last two weeks living in turmoil. She was angry with herself; how could she have been so stupid? She allowed herself to get so caught up in her love life that she almost found herself arrested and on the front page of every tabloid. Then to top off her stupidity, she had just walked away and left Cam sitting there in her car alone, and for what? She had used the excuse of Hollywood, and that was part of it, of course it was; she couldn't ignore that she would be putting herself out there, but it was more than that. She had scared herself, scared herself with how much she had fallen for Camryn and how quickly it had happened, and then she had thought about everything she was asking Cam to do for her: to pretend she didn't exist, keep secrets from everyone she knew. To lie to people. How much longer would Cam put up with that? And when it all got too much and she didn't want to lie and pretend any longer, then what? It would hurt much more in the long run; it was better to just cut her losses now and let Cam move on, wasn't it?

She had cried solidly for four days. Every time Camryn had called her she had wanted to answer and beg for forgiveness, but then what? This was what would happen every time anyone came close to working it out, and it was becoming more and more difficult to hide; she had fallen for Cam, she couldn't deny it. She was head over heels in love with her, but all she was going to end up doing was hurting her.

~Out~

Seeing Cam at the club had been painful beyond words.

178

Her heart ached in her chest; she had never felt pain like it. It was all her own fault, so she couldn't complain about it because there was nothing she could do about it either now. Cam had arrived with a woman. She had moved on already, and it burned her to the core to see it so up close and personal. Watching as someone else leant in and kissed her, those same soft lips that until two weeks ago had been solely hers to kiss. When she imagined the night they must have spent together, she felt lightheaded and had to sit down.

She hadn't known until the previous Friday that they would be filming here; if she had read her script like she was supposed to, then she would have seen the location details printed at the top like they always were, but she hadn't. And once she had realised, well she had assumed it would be okay, because the club didn't open Mondays and Cam usually had that day off anyway. So, when the gorgeous blonde roared in on her bike her heart had leapt, the memory of being on that very bike with her imminent in her mind for just a few seconds until her mind acknowledged the other rider with her, clinging to her.

It was intoxicating as she observed the manager they had earlier been introduced to as Erin walk outside and confront Cam about something she couldn't quite hear. Her heart skipped a beat as Cam angrily began to strip, her leathers being pulled from her body, leaving her clad in only her underwear for all to see. God how she missed that body, warm and firm against her in bed. It was like a car crash that she couldn't turn away from; no matter the pain it caused her, she couldn't stop herself from watching her ex-lover. She winced at the thought of that, that Camryn Thomas was now her ex. But that was nothing to the pain she felt when their eyes met and she noted the icy coolness that clouded them. Those beautiful eyes were pained, and it was all because she wasn't brave enough. Camryn had told her once that she wasn't good enough for Michelle. But she was wrong. It was Michelle who was never good enough for her.

When she saw Cam leave the club minutes later, she couldn't help the tears that fell. She scrutinised her as she headed towards her car, not once glancing up. Focused on just getting to her car and getting out of there. She remembered all the times those beautiful blue eyes had held her in their gaze and now, now she wouldn't even look in her direction.

Chapter Twenty-Seven

At 8am the following morning, she found herself sitting in the office of Janice Rashbrook, her agent and oldest friend in the business. Summoned the previous evening, she didn't really remember how she had even gotten here. She vaguely remembered a car arriving and picking her up, a tall blonde guy. Her first thought had been Gavin, that Cam had sent Gavin, but then he pulled his sunglasses off and she realised the eyes were not like Cam's; they were hazel, not blue like Gavin had.

"What the fuck is wrong with you lately?" Janice spoke frankly to Michelle, just like she always did. The short blonde woman took no prisoners where her clients were concerned. They made each other a lot of money, and that meant a lifestyle she had become accustomed to, and she was not going to sit back and allow anything to fuck that up for either of them!

"Nothing, I'm fine." Michelle shrugged as she sat in the comfy leather seat picking at a thread on her top.

"Fine? Really? You call what you look like, fine? Ya look like shit."

"Wow thanks so much, why am I here?" she asked, looking up from her thread to glare at her friend.

"You are here because in the last two weeks I've barely heard from you, every script I've sent you you've ignored, and last night I got a call from Ramos. You've been showing up late, you don't know your lines. This isn't you, so start talking."

Michelle burst into tears. It felt like that was all she did lately: cry.

"Jesus Michelle, come on, it's just a few scripts," she said, walking over and wrapping her in her arms. "Honey, what's wrong?"

"I can't...I can't do this." She buried her face in her hands and leant forward.

"Do what Honey? I've known you for nearly twenty years and I've never seen you like this. Whatever it is, you can tell me."

Michelle took a tissue from the box Janice offered her and wiped at her eyes. She blew her nose and took in a deep breath to steady herself.

"I can't tell you," she finally croaked, her voice tight with emotion.

"Michelle, look at me. I have never shared anything you tell me with anyone, that's not my job. My job is to protect you, to keep you employed and earning the best you can. It pays me to make sure that you and I have a relationship of trust."

Michelle looked her friend in the eye and knew she was speaking the truth. "I fell in love," she said quickly, then held her breath and waited.

"Ok, see that's not so bad." Janice smiled as she reached for a pot of coffee and poured two fresh cups. "So, what did the bastard do?" she inquired as she passed a cup to Michelle and took a seat.

"Nothing, it was all me, I ended things," she said, as the tears began to fall again.

"Well just call him up and tell him you were wrong,

what man could say no to you when you turn it on."

With that Michelle began to sob once more, chest-heaving cries that had Janice panicking that something untoward had gone on. "Michelle, did he hurt you honey?" she asked, rushing back to her side and kneeling down next to her.

"No! God, Janice you don't understand."

"Then help me to understand, cos I'm real worried about you right now sweetie." Michelle hid her face in her hands again, unable to look at her friend, terrified she would know just by looking at her.

"Please don't make me tell you." Saying it out loud to someone else would make it all too real, it could never be taken back.

"Honey, if he did something then I need to know so we can deal with it properly." Janice gently stroked a hand down Michelle's back.

"Nobody hurt me," she whispered, reminded in an instant at just how beautiful her relationship with Camryn had been. Loving and respectful, everything she had ever wanted or needed from a partner, and she had thrown it away.

"Ok good, then why all the tears and fucking up at work?"

"I...Oh God Jan, I'm...It isn't – it's not what you think."

"So, explain it to me then, Shelly."

Taking a deep breath, Michelle finally made a decision that would probably end her career.

"It's not a man!"

"What isn't?"

"I...I'm not in love...with a man," she whispered. Her head bowed and eyes closed; she felt shame and embarrassment at her inability to not be fearful.

"Oh...*oh!*" Janice repeated, understanding finally what she was telling her.

"Yes *oh*!! Now do you understand?" she almost shouted as she watched Janice continue to stare at her. She prepared herself for the onslaught she expected to hear, and when it didn't come she began to worry even more. Silence was never good. Janice was sitting staring at her, her fingers steepled as she considered what she had just heard from her number one client.

"No, no I don't understand Michelle, if you're in love with her then why the hell are you so unhappy?"

"Because I ended it."

"Why?"

"Why? Why? Why do you think why?" Michelle was confused now and just wanted to get the hell out of there. Embarrassed, frightened, and finding it difficult to comprehend what she had just done, she could feel her heart beating faster.

"I don't know honey, I assumed if she made you happy you wouldn't have ended it, so there must be a better reason."

Michelle couldn't believe this, she had been fretting over this her entire life and now here she was finally telling someone, someone in the business, someone with the power to end her career and...nothing!

"Janice! I just told you I'm gay!" she virtually shrieked.

"Yes dear, so is half of Hollywood, what do you want me to say?" she said with a shrug as she knelt beside the brunette, soothingly patting her hand. She reminded Michelle of her mother a little; they looked nothing like each other, but her actions and her words comforted her.

"So, you're ok with that, you're saying it makes no difference!" Michelle stared deeply into Jan's green eyes. Sincerity and trust were all she could see there.

"I'm saying that half the men and women in Hollywood are gay sweetie, we just manage the hype. Some people find it works in their favour to come out and they enjoy a certain kind of celebrity. Others prefer to keep it private. We just need to work out what's best for you."

Michelle nearly fainted with the relief, but then a new wave of tears begun as she realised what she had lost once more. "You're saying I don't have to hide this? Her?" Michelle asked incredulously.

"Not if you don't want to, but it's probably best to at least be discreet about it, it is your private life after all," Janice said as she walked back to her desk and sat down in the ergonomically-built leather chair she had just bought from a very expensive online store.

Michelle burst into tears once more, soul-shuddering sobs.

"Ok, ok, now I thought we just cleared this up, why are

you crying again?" Janice was beginning to feel like a jack-in-a-box, she was up and down that much.

"Because I've ruined everything."

"How so? Michelle, you can fix this, if she loves you then she will understand." She passed the tissues to her once more. Michelle pulled one out and dabbed her eyes.

"I doubt she loves me. It was very brief, intense but brief and then ... then I panicked and I walked away and she already met someone else...Oh God, what have I done? Camryn will never forgive me."

"Camryn? Camryn who?" It was an unusual name and in this business, names were her game.

"Camryn Thomas, you won't know—"

"I know Cam, she sits on the board of an arts charity I'm also on and if I recall, Camryn Thomas doesn't date. I remember Alice Starberg flirting with her non-stop one afternoon and she brushed it off, I asked her why and she said and I quote that she had 'Been there, done that and more than once is dangerous to one's mental health.'" She used her fingers to indicate quotations marks.

"Exactly so, she won't want me back," she said. "Wait, Alice Starberg? Really?" Alice was an A-list star in anyone's world, she had no idea that she swung both ways.

Janice ignored the remark and kept on point by asking. "How many dates did she take you on?"

"I don't know, a few."

186

"You went on a few dates with someone that 'only' goes on one date and you think she isn't interested?" She laughed loudly and shook her head sardonically.

Michelle stood. "I need to go and I need some time off to get my head together, make it happen please," she said over her shoulder, walking toward the door.

"And we still need to talk about this and work out how to play it."

"Yes, we will, once I know what it is I'm dealing with...Oh and Jan...Thank you!"

Chapter Twenty–Eight

Cam pulled out her suitcase and started packing for her trip. She didn't plan to take much with her, as she had a lot of stuff already there.

Her villa was in a small beach village that overlooked the harbour. It had room to sleep ten people and its own pool; it was lush and green and decorated very much in the Cretan style. She loved it there. It had been a place she had gone to a lot when she was a child, so it held good memories and best of all, none of them included Michelle. She hoped this would mean she could get her out of her system once and for all.

"Maria?" she shouted, trying to locate her housekeeper, her friend.

"Stop shouting, I'm just here," Maria answered back as she came walking around the corner and straight into Cam's room. "What are you doing now? I tidy your stuff up and you just make more mess," she said, marching around the room and picking up items of clothing that Cam had rejected from her packing. The third thing she picked up was a half empty bottle of Grey Goose vodka that she held between finger and thumb as if it were contaminated. She placed it in the trash can.

"I am going away for a bit. So, you're in charge around here, ok?" Cam slurred slightly, the half empty bottle having been her breakfast.

"What are you talking about? I am always in charge around here! Where you going now? Always dashing about somewhere and never just sitting."

"Yes well that may well be true but it doesn't change anything," she argued searching her drawer for her passport. "Have you seen my passport?"

"It's where it should be, in the safe."

"Oh. Great, thanks," she said, moving to her closet and opening the cupboard that housed her small house safe. She leant against the wall to support herself, feeling a little dizzy with the effects of the vodka.

"Camryn, what are you doing?" Maria asked, sitting on the edge of Cam's bed and clasping her hands together in her lap. Cam poked her head out of the closet and then came out and sat next to her.

"I don't know." she said, shaking her head. "But I have to do something. I can't keep doing this." She looked around for the bottle and pointed to it.

Maria said a silent prayer of thanks that Cam had finally said it out loud. "Don't be gone too long ok?"

~Out~

Her taxi arrived on time, so she wheeled her case out and threw it on the backseat and headed for the airport. Fairfield was a smaller airport that she had organised a jet to fly into this morning. It was due to land within the hour and once it did, it would be an hour turn around to restock and refuel and then they would be taking off and heading to Europe.

Chapter Twenty–Nine

Michelle found herself outside of OUT twenty minutes after leaving Janice's office. She noticed Cam's car wasn't there, so she parked in her space. Her heart leapt when she noted the bike, leant to the left on its stand. She crossed her fingers that it meant Camryn was in her office.

Walking inside the club, she had an instant flashback to the stool and the memories that came with it. It tugged at her heart once more to think about just how much she had thrown away that night.

Looking up, she saw Erin watching her as she polished some glasses and placed them one at a time on the counter, clean and shining. The bar looked different in the daytime as Michelle moved quickly to where Erin stood. All the smells and sounds she remembered were gone. Just a clean, open space with a pink haired woman buffing glasses.

"Hi, is Cam here?" Her voice faltered slightly, nerves getting the better of her as she withstood the hard glare coming her way.

"Why?" Erin wasn't in the mood to pay lip service to Michelle right now. She had done enough damage already, and she wasn't going to allow her to continue to play with Cam's emotions. She had never seen Cam anything but happy; witnessing her fall apart was just horrible, and she was tempted to give the actress a piece of her mind.

"I – I need to speak to her, is she here?" She tried to keep her voice steady, but there was something about Erin's demeanour that was wrong. Something was off.

"Nope." Michelle detected a note of hostility in Erin's voice. It was understandable; Cam had obviously told her all about it. That had to be the only explanation to the attitude she was getting right now.

"Look, I don't know what you think you know or care what you think about me, but I need to speak to Camryn, can you give me her address at least?"

"If she hasn't given it to you then I can't either," she answered. Stopping what she was doing, she studied the actress. She looked as bad as Cam did: her eyes were red, and she looked like she hadn't slept for days. "It wouldn't matter anyway, she isn't there," she finally added, starting to feel sorry for the woman.

"I know she probably doesn't want to speak to me and maybe she's told you to get rid of me—"

"She's not here, really...she left this morning," Erin said, interrupting her speech. Seeing the sadness in this one's face too, she could barely stand it. *What was wrong with these idiots?*

"What do you mean, she left?" She didn't like the sound of that at all. It sounded too... permanent.

"Like, she left, packed her bags and left."

Panic started to set in. Michelle's heart raced and she could barely breathe as she grabbed a hold of the counter for support.

"Where...where did she go?"

"Europe," Erin stated. The colour drained instantly from Michelle's face.

"So, I'm too late? ...I'm too late!" she repeated, almost to herself as her legs began to buckle. Erin vaulted the bar and caught her before she could do herself any physical harm.

"Hey, you ok?"

"I'm too late?" she said again, not hearing Erin speaking. "What have I done?"

"You should have asked yourself that two weeks ago when you broke her heart. She's been a mess," Erin said angrily before remembering it wasn't her business and reminding herself that she didn't know all of the details either. She couldn't judge. "Look, it doesn't matter."

"It does, it does matter." Michelle sobbed.

"Why do you want to speak to her now?" Erin demanded.

"I wanted to apologise, but it's too late and now she's gone and I...I miss her." She didn't even care now who knew about them; she was outing herself without even thinking about it.

Erin checked her watch. 9.24 a.m. "Did you drive?"

"Yes, why?"

"You might have time; she doesn't take off until eleven. If you get to the airport you might be able to talk to her."

"I'll never make it to LAX in time."

"She won't be flying from there. Fairfield is where she usually flies out from. We could be there in 40 minutes."

"We?"

"Well you're in no fit state to drive right now, gimme your keys, let's go," Erin said as she stood and pulled Michelle up with her, dragging her along behind her.

"You're helping me?"

"No, I'm helping Cam. Regardless of whatever it is you have done, she needs you and you need to fix her."

Michelle followed behind her in autopilot and waited while Erin locked up the club. She held out her keys, which Erin took from her without a word and climbed into the driver seat of Michelle's X5. "Nice car."

"You get me to the airport before she leaves and it's yours!" Michelle said, clambering in to the passenger seat.

"Are you serious?"

"Serious as a heart attack." Michelle smiled, nervously. Whatever happened from now on, she at least had a chance. If it cost her a $72k black BMW SUV then so be it; it was a price she would willingly pay.

Erin drove and Michelle prayed. Cars and people, houses and buildings all passed by in a blur as Erin put her foot down as best she could and tried to dodge around the traffic that slowly moved. She had lived here for a long time and she knew a lot of roads that she could use to keep her off the main routes. They cruised along until they had no choice but to join the 405. Traffic was busy and the five lanes were slow, but it was moving at least, slowly but surely.

Erin pulled into the airport at exactly 10:35 a.m. They both ran inside the building and found a help desk. Michelle quickly explained that she needed to catch Camryn Thomas with some important business before she left for Europe.

"Ma'am, you will need to sign in, and I will need to see some ID."

"Fine, ok, yes I can do that. Where do I sign in?" Michelle spoke quickly, her eyes darting across the desk for the form she needed to sign. She thanked Erin while she rummaged in her bag and pulled out her driver's license.

The receptionist informed them that somebody would be down shortly to show her through to the waiting room where Camryn would be. "Thank you," Michelle said, sincerity lacing her words as she held out a hand for Erin.

"No problem. Just be honest with her," Erin advised. She waved as the guard they were waiting for arrived to escort Michelle. Following him, she went back outside and along a walkway that led past several other buildings housing smaller planes, tiny little two-seaters and a few helicopters. He continued on until they reached a larger building at the farther end. She could see on the tarmac that bigger planes were parked up, people moving around them as they were being readied.

Entering the building, she struggled to keep up with him. He was clearly used to the walk and knew where he was going, his stride long and confident. Eventually he stopped outside a door that read 'waiting room'. That was where he left her. She took a breath to steady herself before opening the door, to an empty room!

Pushing the door open fully, she entered the small room and closed the door behind her. Two red couches angled together with a table in the corner between them sitting neatly on top of a beautiful thick carpet. Fresh coffee filled the air with its invigorating aroma flooding the senses, but the room was empty. She was too late. Her legs gave way as she slid down the door and sobbed into her hands, unable to contemplate just what she could do next.

From the other side of the room, the bathroom door opened and Camryn stepped back into the small waiting room. She took in the sight before her. *Hallucinating now, you're obsessed Thomas. Let it go.*

Becoming aware there was someone else in the room, Michelle slowly raised her head, peeking out from between her fingers. Standing on the opposite side of the room was the haunted presence of her lover.

"Cam?" she whispered hoarsely, barely audible. The blonde ignored her and took the steps towards a plush sofa where she flopped down, her head falling backwards and her eyes squeezed shut. *And now I'm hearing things.*

"Camryn, please," Michelle continued as she stood on shaky legs. She wasn't sure she would make it across the room, but she was damn well going to try. For the first time, she noticed the empty miniature bottles of vodka scattered on the table next to her.

Cam opened her eyes and looked up at the hallucination. "You're not real, I'm just tired and drunk," she slurred as she tried to focus her eyes.

"Camryn I am real, please Cam. It's me, please, can we talk?" she pleaded; she would plead all day long if she had to. It was a fragile moment and she did not want to spook her. Cam looked awful. Black rings darkened under her eyes, she looked so tired, drawn and thinner; she was definitely thinner, but with more muscle definition somehow. *God, what have I done to this woman?*

"Cam, can you look at me? I want – no, I need to apologise."

Silence. She moved closer, as close as she dared before dropping to her haunches in front of Camryn. She smelt so good; she had missed this closeness, being able to lay eyes on her, but it wasn't enough without being able to touch her again.

"Cam? Baby, please." She reached out a hand but withdrew it immediately.

"Baby?" Cam scoffed, an ironic laugh bubbling up and out of her throat. "I'm not your baby. Not now, not anymore. You left me! Yep, you!" She pointed at her, poking the air with her finger to every word she uttered. "You left me sitting in my car outside your gates. You – you just walked away without even saying goodbye," she angrily spat out. "Just walked away!" she emphasised, her voice a higher-pitched singsong. "Like I was nothing to you." She finally hissed.

Michelle swallowed. "I know, I know I did and I'm so sorry I did that to you. You didn't deserve that. I – I got scared and I – I don't know why I did that, only that I did do it and I'm so sorry and ashamed. I don't want you to leave without knowing that I wish I hadn't hurt you." She cried, the tears flowing freely down her cheeks. Her heart ached and she closed her eyes, unable to look at what she had done.

The door to her left suddenly opened and a man in uniform stepped inside carrying a small flight bag. He was tall with close-cropped sandy hair and a smiling face. His white shirt was pressed perfectly, not a crease in sight, and he was holding a hat under his arm.

"Ms Thomas, we are ready to board as soon as you are—" He looked from one woman to the other realising he was interrupting something. "Oh, I wasn't informed you would be having a guest on board. It's not a problem, if I can just have any passport details then I can correct our flight details, we should be taking off in approximately fifteen minutes." He waited for a reply and without getting one he quickly added, "I'll see you on the jet." He then made a hasty exit and left them alone once more.

"Why are you here?" Cam spoke quietly. She sounded almost childlike, her voice, usually so strong and loud, now nothing more than a whisper, as though the words themselves hurt too much to say.

"I needed to tell you." Michelle dropped to her knees and pressed her palms together in prayer to try and stop herself from reaching for her again.

"Tell me what?" The icy glare she gave caused a shiver to make its way down Michelle's spine. Those beautiful blue orbs were trying so desperately not to look at her with the love she still felt.

"I love you, I love you Camryn."

"No! You don't love me," she said, shaking her head at Michelle. "People that love one another don't do what you did. I did everything you asked me to do but it wasn't enough, it was never enough. I wasn't enough. I should have known, it's my own fault, I was stupid to think it could be any different." A solitary tear slid lonely down her cheek and she made no move to wipe it away, its trail a reminder of its existence, of her heart's existence.

"No, no, you weren't, it was never you," Michelle shouted, cutting her off and reaching for her hand, pulling away again at the last moment when Cam flinched, not wanting to be touched. "*I* was stupid, I was so stupid to think that anything was more important than you, don't you see? I'm not frightened anymore, I don't care who knows about us."

"And what makes you think I still care?" Cam said callously, as she finally locked eyes with her, the ice-cold stare absent of any further emotion.

Michelle was taken aback. The thought that Cam no longer cared was like a scalpel to her heart, clean and precise in its incision. But what else could she expect? Cam had already been with another woman, maybe more. What if she really had moved on?

"I'm sorry, I shouldn't have assumed that you still did." She looked away, unable to witness the complete reversal of feeling in those eyes when they looked at her, eyes that until now had always looked at her with love and reverence.

"I can't, I can't care about you! I can't do this again. Jessica was bad enough, but you? I can't. It's too much, it's too hard," Cam muttered, more to herself than Michelle. She stood up and grabbed her bag. "I have to go. Goodbye Ms Hamlin."

Chapter Thirty

When Michelle all but staggered outside, she found Erin waiting by the car. It wasn't that much longer until the loud rumble of an aircraft taking off thundered above them and her eyes were drawn to the ascending plane as Camryn Thomas left the United States, taking Michelle's heart with her.

"You're still here?" Michelle said, barely believing that Cam's right-hand woman would have waited for her. She had fully expected her and the car to be long gone; after all, a promise was a promise.

"I figured I'd wait around, just in case," Erin said, her pink hair fluttering in the breeze. "She can be a stubborn fuck sometimes," she added, referring to her boss. "Come on, get in. I'll take you home."

Michelle did as she was told, the fight no longer in her to argue. And anyway, what was the point; where else was there for her to go now? She had behaved selfishly and then made the assumption that she could just decide all was ok again and that Camryn would come running back to her.

The journey was quiet. Erin tried for some small talk, but it was clear that Shelly Hamlin was too distraught and not in the mood for it. So, she kept her eyes facing forward, guiding the car through the traffic and back down towards the beach. Michelle gave her the name of the street they needed when she was asked, but otherwise her thoughts were elsewhere.

"Do you love her?" Erin asked. They had just turned into Michelle's street, the rows of parked cars narrowing the lane.

She glanced quickly across at the actress. Her deep brown eyes filled with tears as she nodded.

"Yes," she whispered. Erin pulled up in front of the gates and turned to face her, scrutinising her with her narrowed eyes.

"Would you do anything to get her back?" Again Michelle nodded. Slowly, unsure where this was going, she turned in her seat. "She is the nicest person I know. Decent, ya know? And I gotta be honest here, if she is this hurt and upset with you then I dunno if you even deserve my help but, I know you are the only one that can fix this." Erin could see the cogs in Shelly's brain whirring away as she tried to piece together what it was that Erin was proposing. "She came here for a reason, running from something or someone back home. She never talks about it but we all know there's a story there."

Michelle reached across the console and hit a button attached to her keys. The gates began to move apart.

"And now she's running from you. You're haunting her and she can't deal with it so, you need to fix it."

Michelle thought back to her conversation with Cam earlier. She had mentioned a Jessica, that it *was bad enough with Jessica*. Whatever this Jessica had done had caused Camryn to flee her home, to leave behind everything and everyone she knew to start a new life here, and now here she was creating the same storm to rage in her once more. What if she created a new life somewhere else now?

"What do I have to do?" she asked as Erin drove through the gates and parked the vehicle to the side.

"Find her. Make her understand that you're sorry. Make

it all ok in her mind so that she can come back here to her life...with or without you," Erin explained. "If you seriously love her like you say you do then you have to show her the way back from this and be prepared to lose her anyway. That's what love is!"

"How?"

"I dunno how—"

"No I mean how? How do I show her if she is in another country and won't speak to me?" Michelle argued, turning away. "She wouldn't even look at me."

Erin thought for a minute. She hadn't known Cam long in the great scheme of things, but she had worked with her on a daily basis for over a year and she had seen her interact with hundreds of people. "She's in love with you. Any fool can see it and whatever you did...Look, before you there was nobody, and I mean *nobody,* that she looked at the way she looked at you that night in the bar. I mean she has had...She hasn't been a saint, there have been women, but not one has come close to getting anywhere near her like you did. She's hurt and unhappy but also, she is pissed. She let you in and...now she doesn't know how to push you out. So, while you're still in there, you have a chance. While her heart still wraps itself around you..."

"I need to find her." Michelle said, "How can I find her?"

"Get a bag packed and I'll be back. There is only one woman who will know where she is and have the address." Erin smiled at the thought of Maria and then the image of her dishtowel popped and she considered if all of this was worth it.

Chapter Thirty-One

Erin knocked hard on the door of Camryn's beach house. The door swung open and the diminutive woman behind it looked up and smiled at her guest.

"Erin, come in, come in." The smile on her face lit up as she stepped aside and made room for Camryn's colourful friend to enter the house. "Camryn isn't here, did she not tell you?"

"Yeah, she told me. She told me why as well." Erin followed her into the kitchen and took up a seat at the breakfast table. Maria poured coffee and joined her. "I have a plan but...I need your help."

"Tell me what it is?"

~Out~

An hour later and Erin was pulling back inside the gates of Shelly Hamlin's Brentwood home with a scrap of paper in her pocket. The actress opened the door and just like Maria had, she moved aside to allow Erin to enter.

She had changed while Erin was gone, now wearing blue jeans and a lightweight jumper that hung loosely at the neck. Her hair was tied back and she was barefooted. There was a case by the door along with a handbag and a pair of shoes.

"Good, you're ready to go?"

"Yes. As ready as I can be considering I have no idea where I am going." She spoke quietly, almost defeated. She had spent the last hour or so wandering the house with no real idea of what to pack or do. In the end she opted for the basics. She was trying to be positive, trying to imagine that Cam would forgive her and they could enjoy a couple of days together at least, but then the negative thoughts would reappear when she remembered just how cold Cam's eyes were when she had looked at her and told her goodbye.

"I got the address. Can you just fly out like this?" Erin was concerned. It was one thing trying to fix Camryn, but at Shelly Hamlin's expense? She wasn't so sure Cam would be happy about that. She wasn't that sure how happy she would be to find out that Maria and herself had had such an input in the idea to send Shelly to her either. If it went wrong, they could both find themselves out of a job. Maria had been confident that that wouldn't happen, but Erin wasn't so sure.

"Yes, I spoke with my agent. She has gotten me out of some interviews and I'm not needed now on *Medical Diaries*; it goes on hiatus next week until the New Year. I just have a film coming up, but right now, I am free for a few weeks."

"Ok. So, there's a flight out of LAX in a few hours. It's a ten-hour flight to London and then you have to change there. From there it's another four hours on to a place called Chania, in Crete. It's a tight connection time, but it's doable. There is also the time difference to consider. You'll need to sleep as much as you can on the plane."

"Alright, I'll see if I can book the ticket." Michelle didn't care how difficult it would be; she was going.

"I already did. Cam left me a credit card, so I called ahead and booked you on the flight. You can pick the tickets up when you get there." Erin started walking towards the door. "Come on, I'll drop you off." She picked up the suitcase and waited at the door. For a moment she didn't think Shelly Hamlin would follow, but she did.

Chapter Thirty-Two

Cam arrived in Crete at 8 a.m. local time. The private jet had allowed for a certain level of comfort that meant she had been able to enjoy at least a few hours of sleep. She felt better physically. She had sobered up for one, and the headache that had started to develop was now just a dull thud as the painkillers kicked in. Exhausted emotionally still, she just needed to relax. Get to the villa and chill out. Sleep some more and lay around the pool for as long as it took.

Walking away from Michelle and climbing the steps to the jet had been the hardest thing she had ever done, but she had to do it. Regardless of what Cam felt for the actress, she couldn't just roll over and let it go. She was nobody's doormat.

It had been a long flight with a stopover in Copenhagen for fuel. Her dreams were haunted by brown eyes and dimples whenever she closed her eyes, but at least she had managed those crucial few hours.

She took a taxi from the airport and was in her villa and unpacked by midday (Greek time). She had barely noticed the journey through the towns and villages that led to the motorway and then back down to the village she lived in. The driver had tried to converse with her, and she had managed a few words of Greek that she remembered. As a child, she came here every year, and each time the local shop owner would refuse to serve her unless she learnt a new Greek word or phrase. Gradually, she had picked up enough to get by.

They were familiar surroundings and they helped to

ground her. Established walls and firm flooring beneath her feet made it a welcome relief. Grabbing a bottle of water from the fridge, she wandered out onto the patio and looked out across the pool to regard the view; the sea was as blue as it had ever been. She sipped the cool liquid as she admired the sky and the way the breeze banished every cloud that dared to cross its path. The sun hung high in the sky, hot already, just waiting for bare flesh to scorch. There was barely any noise, just the distant sound of waves and the breeze. Occasionally a voice would rise above the silence, but mainly it was quiet and just what Cam needed.

She kicked off her shoes and pulled her socks off, the stone warm on her soles as she walked toward the pool. It looked too inviting to ignore as she felt the heat on her face. So she stripped off her clothes and then, naked, dove right in.

The water was deceptively cold. Her body temperature warmer from the sun's rays, it felt like she had dived into a giant melting ice cube, but it was refreshing and woke her up. As she began to swim and the water warmed, her thoughts began to disentangle. Back and forth she swam, gaining speed and rhythm.

She swam until she exhausted herself. Unable to finish another length, she floated towards the steps and climbed out, almost staggering back to the villa, her clothes left where she had taken them off. Still naked, she dropped down onto her bed and as her mind finally cleared, too exhausted to think any longer, she fell into a deep sleep.

Chapter Thirty–Three

Cam had had a six-hour head start, and with a thirty minute delay at LAX, Michelle had barely made her connection. It was almost dark by the time she touched down on the Greek island. Originally booked in an economy class seat, she had spent the first few hours of the journey cramped and uncomfortable, that is until one of the stewards recognised her and discreetly offered her an upgrade. She willingly paid the extra to stretch out in a bigger seat, and once settled she was able to sleep a little. She asked the same steward if he could wake her in three hours. With the time difference, she didn't want to sleep the entire journey and be wide awake all night once she got there. She needed to be alert and ready for anything because there was no guarantee that Cam was going to be happy to see her or even allow her to stay.

She handed the piece of paper that Maria had written the address down on to the taxi driver; he spoke limited English but was very excited that she was an American. He explained all about the American naval base, she thought he said at Souda, but she wasn't so sure, so she just nodded and smiled appropriately.

Eventually he pulled off from the motorway and they made their way down toward the coast. She could smell the sea air the closer they got and when they were finally heading along the road parallel to the beach, she tried to take everything in: all the restaurants that were lit up and alive with music and people talking and laughing. It was lively without being too crazy. This clearly wasn't where the 18-30s came for a fun and alcohol-fuelled break.

It was a little surreal. She was in Greece. Not even 24 hrs ago she was at Fairfield pleading with Camryn, and now here she was following her halfway around the world. Her thoughts were interrupted when the taxi took a firm turn to the left and went up a short but steep hill until it took another sharp turn to the left and stopped abruptly in front of a pair of black iron gates. She climbed out and noted she could just walk around them; they were only there to stop vehicles from entering the property.

The driver placed her bag on the floor beside the gate and told her the price of the fare. She congratulated herself on at least having had the foresight to swap out some dollars for Euros when she had reached LAX. She paid him, along with a hefty tip.

As he backed away from the gates, the light lessened and, taking a breath, she quickly grabbed her bags and started the walk up to the big house. There were some small lights that edged the pathway, but it was pretty dark as she wheeled her case behind her. All that greeted her was the happy chirping of the cicada and the odd buzz of a mosquito as it danced around the light.

There was a light on at the patio, so she followed that and walked right up to an open door. The lights inside were off, the entire house in complete darkness. She wasn't sure what to do next.

"Cam?" she called out quietly. "Camryn?" Nothing, there was no movement. She considered that maybe the blonde had gone out; maybe it was different over here and unlocked doors were the norm.

Leaving her suitcase where it was, she wandered inside,

flicking the light on as she went. The room she entered by was the kitchen, compact but with everything it needed. It led through to an open plan lounge and dining area with a table and chairs for at least ten people. Every wall was whitewashed. Blue curtains that looked as though they had hung there for forty years framed the windows. It was rustic and not at all how Michelle pictured any house that Camryn would own. But it was homely and warm. There were three steps that headed downward, to the left a corridor that ran further into the building, doors on either side as well as the end of the hallway.

Gingerly she stepped down them and along the hall. Coming to the first door on the right, she opened it and found an empty room. The bed was made ready for a guest, but that was all. Opposite was a door that lead to the bathroom, a tiled wet room with a shower cubicle, sink and toilet. Opening the second door on the right, she almost gasped at the sight before her.

Camryn lay naked on her front, above the covers, her bare backside slightly paler than the rest of her. Michelle had to bite her lip to avoid speaking out loud. She wanted to reach out and touch her, take all of her own clothes off and climb into bed beside her, pull her close and never let her go again. Instead, she backed out quietly and closed the door.

Chapter Thirty-Four

Feeling chilled from the damp bedclothes and the cooler air as darkness fell, Camryn awoke feeling a little out of sync. As she stood up and stretched, she thought for just a second that she could smell Michelle. She sniffed the air and shook her head. *Stop imagining things.*

Her wardrobe held a good selection of clothes, so she pulled out a top and some jogging bottoms. Yanking them on, she realised just how famished she was. She couldn't remember the last time she ate anything she had enjoyed. Maria had been leaving food in the fridge for her to heat up but she hadn't, choosing to drink the vodka instead.

Opening the door to her room, she got the distinct waft of toast and fresh coffee as she walked the corridor back into the lounge. Tying the drawstring on her joggers, she heard a noise and cocked her ear. There was a tinkling sound as though somebody had stirred a spoon in a mug. She came to a dead halt, alert and ready to pound anyone that had had the nerve to break into her house and steal...*toast*? It didn't make sense. As she rounded the corner and looked into the kitchen, she saw the room was empty.

Feeling a little foolish, she ran her fingers through her hair and smiled to herself. *You really are cracking up.*

And then she noticed the coffee pot, half full with dark liquid. She hadn't made any coffee since she had been here, but it was warm to the touch. Crumbs lay haphazardly on the chopping board, along with a knife and the loaf of bread she had organised with Vana as part of her arrival package.

The village shop owner was a long-time friend, and anytime Camryn came here she would email ahead and Vana would deliver her the essentials. She had a key to the property and kept an eye on it, organising the pool boy and the cleaner to pop in weekly and give it all the once over. Every month she sent the gardener in to tidy the flower beds and cut the grass. It was one less thing for Camryn to worry about; all she had to do was send the money needed to pay them all. In return, Vana got to use any of Cam's other properties for her own vacations.

The sharp scraping of a chair from outside brought her attention back to the present and she realised that she did indeed have a guest; wanted or not, somebody was on her property, was in her house. They had made themselves at home and were now relaxing on her patio.

She stepped outside into the fresh evening air and there, sitting modestly on a chair, coffee cup in hand, was Michelle.

~Out~

"Sleep well?" the brunette asked nonchalantly as she sipped her coffee and looked up at the blonde standing in the doorway. Cam wasn't sure what to say to that. She looked around her and then regarded the actress once more. She was sober now. She was rested, and this was not a figment of her imagination.

"What are you doing here?" she asked calmly before shaking her head. "Actually no, how did you get here?"

"On a plane, same as you. Not quite so comfortably, of course, but it got me here." She placed her cup down on the table. "Would you like some coffee?" She stood up, walked past Camryn and into the house as though she owned it and had always been here. Camryn watched her. She opened the correct cupboard door and pulled down a mug, moved to the fridge and claimed the milk. This was all wrong.

"No, you can't be here," Cam said from behind her. Michelle stiffened imperceptibly before continuing with her task, pouring the coffee, adding the milk, and stirring. She turned then and walked past Camryn back outside, placing the cup on the table opposite where her own sat next to a plate of crumbs. Without a word, she sat back down and lifted her particular cup to her lips, taking a sip.

"Well, I am here and I am not leaving."

"I don't want you here. This is trespassing, I'll just call the police—"

"Go ahead. However, I am not leaving. I will just come back again in the morning, and the afternoon, and wherever you go I will follow until you forgive me."

Cam scoffed at that. "Forgive you? Have you lost your mind?"

"Yes, forgive me. I love you and I am not leaving until you realise that. I am not leaving here or you until you comprehend that this wasn't your fault."

Cam considered that, took a seat, and contemplated it a little more before finally working through her thoughts enough to speak again.

"What you don't or won't understand is that I know whose fault it is. I am well aware of your choice to toss me aside and ignore me like I never existed." She noted the flush of discomfiture that crawled up the calm exterior Michelle was portraying. "What your feelings for me are now is of no matter. Because I don't want it." It was a lie and they both knew it. She stood and walked to the edge of the patio, not daring to look at the brunette a moment longer.

"Ok, you can tell yourself that all you want, we both know it isn't true Camryn. You love me." She waited until Camryn finally turned and looked at her once more before she continued. "I got scared and I let my fears overwhelm me and I ruined the best fucking thing to happen to me! I know that!" She paused, her tone lowering. "I miss you."

"You miss me? What do you miss about me exactly? Because you didn't seem to miss me much when I was calling and texting to talk to you." She glared at Michelle, daring her to speak again. "When I needed you!"

Standing, Michelle softened her voice, not wanting to escalate this conversation into an argument; she needed to make Cam see that she was being candid. She saw the change in her eyes; the heated exchange had thawed the ice.

"I missed you every day. Every minute of every day. I miss everything! I miss how you touch me. I miss how you speak to me. I miss how I know you will always be there for me. I miss *you*! I miss that even now, when you're trying so hard to be angry with me, you can't look at me with anything but love in your eyes." She paused, her eyes set upon Camryn with intent. "I miss how you look at me. I miss how you kiss me." Her voice laced with emotion and on the verge of tears, she slumped down into the chair Cam had vacated.

Cam tore her eyes from her and began walking away. Then she stopped and turned back on her heels to face her.

"You don't get to pick and choose when you can love me! You can't just turn up and say all the right things and it all be ok, it doesn't work like that!" She walked back to where Michelle sat. "You're right, I can't look at you with anything but love in my eyes, because I never stopped. I didn't walk away at the first opportunity," she fumed, her voice raised.

"No, but you moved on pretty quickly, didn't you?" Michelle yelled back. "Huh? Didn't take you long to move someone else into your bed the minute I was gone."

"What does that have to do with anything?" Cam screamed. "You left me! You walked away without even a goodbye." Michelle fell silent. Because when all was said and done, it all came back to that. She had walked away, and she had no right to complain about anything Camryn chose to do after that.

"I'm sorry." Her voice was lower and calmer now. "I wish with all my heart that I hadn't done that, but I did and I can't take it back Camryn. If you give me a chance, then I'll prove to you how much I really do love you."

The darkness she had found herself sucked into over the last two weeks or so had been a shock to her system; even when she had split with Jessica, she hadn't felt like this. She had been too busy trying to keep a roof over her head to have time to fall into a depression, and then when she had won all that money, she suddenly had a lot of other interests to enjoy instead of thinking about Jessica. Yes, it had hurt her deeply, but it wasn't losing Jessica that had really been the problem; it was the sense of betrayal, the loss of trust with Kate. This though, this was different; Michelle was different. What she felt for Michelle was much stronger than anything she had ever felt for anyone. Which is why it hurt much more.

"I'm struggling to understand what more I could have done to make you happy?" Cam looked at her now, tears forming as she waited for an answer. "Because that's the problem Michelle. *I* can't make you happy. *I* can't make you like who you are. And I can't make it ok for you to love me."

"You don't need to. I spoke to Janice, I told her everything, and she is fine with it." Michelle smiled, relieved at finally being able to tell Cam that it would all be ok.

"So Janice says it's ok? What about you!? I don't need Janice's approval, I needed yours," she argued. "It's ok then if I post a photograph of us kissing on Twitter? Is that what you're saying?"

"What? No, why would you do that?"

Cam shook her head and laughed at the look of panic on Michelle's face. "You're right, this is only going to hurt more in the long run. So, it's best to just cut our losses now. I'll organise a flight home for you in the morning." Cam stood and walked inside the house, leaving Michelle to contemplate that it really was over.

Chapter Thirty-Five

A fitful night's sleep was the least of Michelle's problems when she woke early the following morning. She listened hard, but couldn't hear any sounds in the house to indicate that Camryn was awake. It was almost silent but for the breeze blowing the trees nearer the house. Her room overlooked the back of the property where the orange and lemon trees grew in a small orchard.

Cam wanted her gone, that was what her words had said, but Michelle knew differently in her heart. It was always in her eyes, the way that she looked at Michelle; she couldn't hide it.

So, for the second day running, she needed a plan, because she was not leaving.

Getting up and dressed quickly, she moved around the villa as quietly as she could. She grabbed a book from the shelf and wandered out to the pool. Finding the area that basked the most in the early morning sunlight, she dropped her robe and made herself comfortable on the lounger with her cup of coffee on the table next to her.

~Out~

The first thing Camryn did when she woke up was to send Erin an email. She wanted to know what the hell had gone on and how the fuck did Michelle know where to find her? She made threats to fire her and anyone else involved in undermining her, and then she called up Steven and organised for him to book Michelle on the next available flight. She got pissy with him when he told her the next flight would not be until later that night.

Fed up and confused with her emotions, she finally got out of bed and trudged into the kitchen. The coffee pot was full again and she sighed, realising that yet again Michelle had made herself at home. Regardless, she poured a cup and wandered outside, scratching the side of her torso where she assumed she had been bitten by a mosquito.

Expecting to find Michelle on the patio as with the previous night, Cam was surprised to see the chairs empty. She took a sip of her coffee and looked further ahead, making a sweep of the pool with her eyes. There she was, in all her glory, laid out on the lounger under a sun hat, book in hand, her face looking toward the sea. She looked exquisite, and Cam took a moment to enjoy the view covertly before she shook herself and remembered what she had to do.

"I've booked you on a flight that leaves at 5 p.m. this evening." Michelle didn't look up from her book or acknowledge that she had even spoken to her. "I said—"
"I ignored you perfectly well the first time," she declared.

"Right well, you can just sit here till then then," Cam countered, feeling somewhat peeved about the whole thing.

"Ok, but just so you're aware," She turned now to face her and slid her sunglasses down her nose just enough that those chocolate browns could be seen in all their sincerity, "I'm not leaving." She then pushed the glasses back in place and returned to her book. Cam sighed.

"Michelle, this isn't up for discussion."

"Correct Camryn." She closed the book and placed it on

the table before standing, the red bikini she wore showing a lot of flesh. She noted the intake of breath that Camryn tried not to show. "I already told you last night. I am not leaving until you forgive me."

"Fine, I forgive you. Ok!" Cam said, her eyes wide with frustration. Michelle smiled and walked toward her. Her finger slid down Cam's cheek and along her bottom lip. Electricity flowed like liquid as it passed from one to the other and back again.

"Good try, Camryn, but we both know that's not true. Now, I am going to get dressed and then I think I'd like you to show me where the local stores are so that I can fill the fridge properly. Ok?" She walked away, leaving Cam speechless and paralysed with a mixture of arousal and exasperation.

~Out~

An hour later and Cam found herself walking into the village with Michelle. She reasoned with herself that regardless of Michelle being here or not, she did actually require more food, and it wasn't like Michelle had anywhere else to be until 5 p.m. It was only eleven now.

"*Kalimera,* Vana," Cam said, smiling at the dark-haired Greek woman who sat on her stool by the till as she wished her a good morning.

"Camryn! I wondered how long until you made it down here?" she said enthusiastically, coming out from behind her counter to hug the blonde she had known for twenty years.

"Yeah, I would have come yesterday but I slept most of it, jet lag is a bitch." She spoke easily to the Greek woman. Short dark hair interspersed with a few grey ones now, she looked so very Greek with her deep tan and dark eyes. She was a few years older than Cam was, but she still looked good for her years.

"Well it's a much longer flight from LA than London huh?" She chuckled and then looked toward the dark-haired women who was standing next to Camryn and watched the lack of interaction with interest. When it became clear to Michelle that Camryn wasn't going to introduce her to her friend, she grabbed a basket and proceeded to mooch around the little store by herself. "You don't introduce your..." The Greek woman wasn't sure which word to use, friend or girlfriend. Cam looked back and around the store to where Michelle was now out of earshot.

"It's complicated and she is leaving later today." Vana looked confused, her eyebrows knitted together.

"You got here yesterday and she's already leaving?! What did you do?" She smiled at her and watched the reactions that moved through the blonde Englishwoman's features. "You ok?"

"Yeah, I guess I'd better see if she needs help," Cam exhaled, jutting her chin at the brunette.

The shop wasn't that big, but it seemed to sell everything you could ever need, much like many similar stores throughout Greece and other European tourist areas. Michelle already had the essentials in the basket: bread, milk and cheese, some tins of stuffed vine leaves, and a jar of olives. The basket looked heavy as she transferred it from one arm to the other.

"Let me take that," Cam said, reaching out for the basket. Their fingers brushed briefly as Michelle attempted to keep hold of it. That electric feeling that passed between them was still evident, if ignored. Every touch, no matter how small, she felt the jolt.

"It's fine," Michelle said. Cam took a leaf out of her book and ignored her, taking the basket anyway. "Thank you." Cam nodded, acknowledging that she had spoken to her.

Vana observed them both as they moved around one another. It was obvious they were in love, both of them taking surreptitious glances at one another when the other wasn't looking, reaching out to one another but then thinking better of it and withdrawing. Every now and then a discussion about something one of them wanted to place in the basket would turn into a brief disagreement, but she felt that it was purely an excuse to talk and look at each other.

"So, all done?" Vana asked as Cam placed the basket in the slanted space for it. She nodded and Michelle smiled at the woman. "Ya know you look a lot like that actress."

Cam stiffened, waiting for Michelle's go to reaction of running the moment anyone recognised her while she was with her.

"Yeah, I get that a lot. It might be because I am that actress." She smiled and held out her hand. "Shelly Hamlin. Lovely to meet you." Vana returned the smile and shook her hand vigorously. Camryn stood, mouth agape. If she hadn't witnessed the entire scene then she wouldn't have believed it.

"Well, it's certainly beats the usual riff-raff we get in here." She tilted her head toward Camryn and both women laughed, bonding over the blonde.

"What do we owe you?" Michelle asked, but the darker-haired women just smiled at her.

"You have to ask in Greek," Cam said, unable to suppress a small smirk, knowing full well that Vana knew already to add it to her bill.

"Oh, well then you will have to teach me," Michelle returned back at Cam, flirting a little. The blonde considered that and seemed to come to a decision pretty quickly.

"*Póso, parakalo?*" Michelle smiled and repeated the phrase back to the Greek woman, who found the whole exchange fascinating as well as entertaining.

"*Eikosi dyo euros, parakalo,*" she answered, indicating the numbers twenty-two on the till.

~Out~

Chapter Thirty-Six

With everything packed away, Cam walked straight into her bedroom and got changed. They had five hours or so before Michelle left, and she was planning to spend the day bathing in the sunshine. Pulling on a black bikini top with matching shorts, she grabbed a towel and a bottle of sunscreen, last of all a pair of bright blue reflective aviators. She checked herself in the mirror and headed back outside via the patio doors to her bedroom, completely circumventing the rest of the house.

She expected to find Michelle out by the pool, pulling some other dirty trick to try and convince her to let her stay, but surprisingly the pool area was empty. She just had the sunshine and a butterfly fluttering about for company.

~Out~

Lying on her back, hands behind her head, aviators on, Cam could hear the slight shuffle of bare feet as they moved across the paved area. There was a tinkling sound as something ceramic was placed on the table and then the scraping of a chair as Michelle finally sat down.

Cam opened one eye. Hidden by her sunglasses, she could see the brunette looking right at her. Waiting.

"Why are you staring at me?" Cam finally asked, not moving an inch.

"I made something to eat," she replied proudly, and then she looked away from the blonde and began to serve herself from the huge salad bowl. Cam continued to lie on her lounger, determined not to join her for lunch. Her stomach, like a traitor, rumbled and gave her away, so she sacrificed her pride and sat up. "Greek salad and bread." Michelle stated, spooning a healthy portion onto a plate for her.

"Thank you," Cam replied. Small cubes of feta cheese crumbled in between huge chunks of tomato and cucumber, while succulent olives glistened and sat comfortably in amongst the rest. It looked delicious, and, taking a quick glance at her companion, so did she. They ate in silence.

When they were finished, Michelle took the plates inside and began to wash them, fully expecting Camryn to stay out by the lounger. When she walked in through the kitchen door behind her, however, Michelle felt her heart skip a beat, her breathing quickening at the nearness of the blonde.

"Why did you tell Vana who you were?" Cam asked as she stood leaning back against the counter behind her. She could read Vana and knew that the woman could tell they were more than just...friends!

"I told you, I spoke to Janice and everything is ok." She continued to wash and rinse, keeping her back to Camryn, but her hopes rose a little.

"But if I suggest a picture on Twit—"

Michelle sucked in a breath and spun around. "No, I don't want pictures of you with me all over social media, not because I am ashamed or scared but because it's my private life and I'd like to have some semblance of control over it." She wiped her hands on the dish towel, threw it on the counter, and stormed past Camryn before turning abruptly. "This is not all about you Camryn! I am entitled to a private life regardless of who I am in love with."

Cam watched her stalk down the steps and off to her room, and for the first time since that fateful night, she actually tried to see things from Michelle's point of view. When they got together Cam had made it clear she was willing to wait and be a secret, so why now did she have this obsession with Michelle coming out and proving something she didn't need her to prove to start with? And to make matters worse, Michelle was making it clear she was prepared to prove it.

It was two thirty and the room felt suddenly cold. Her phone beeped from where it sat on the countertop. Erin had replied. Her first thought was to ignore it and toss it back on the counter, but curiosity got the better of her.

Hey Cam,

I know you're probably going to fire me and I don't blame you I guess. But you should know that what I did came from the right place. She makes you happy and she loves you like nobody else has so I just think you have an opportunity here. Life is too short and yeah she made a mistake, a huge mistake but if you can't see how sorry she is then maybe you don't deserve her anyway.

Ok, so I will continue to do my job until I hear differently

from you.

Good luck with whatever you choose to do and thank you for the opportunity to run this amazing bar and work for you this past year.

Erin.

She placed the phone back down on the counter and rubbed the bridge of her nose between her fingers. She wouldn't fire Erin, that much she knew already, but they would be having a conversation about boundaries in the near future. As well as Maria, because none of this could have happened without her helping the pair of them, and why would Maria have done that, risked breaking that trust they had built up? Unless she really believed Erin was right about Michelle.

Deep down she knew it was true too. Michelle loved her and was sorry. Didn't everybody make mistakes? Had it not been for Jessica, would she have been so sensitive to Michelle hurting her now? If it hadn't been for Jessica she wouldn't have the life she had now, and if it weren't for Michelle, then she would have no understanding of what it was to be in love with someone who felt the same way about her, to feel her heart literally overflowing with love whenever she was anywhere near her. And if Michelle hadn't done what she did, then she would never have had to face the prospect of losing the one thing in life she didn't want to live without: Cam.

Cam growled out loud and stomped down the steps towards the bedroom that Michelle was using. She didn't bother to knock. She just flung the door open and stood looking at the brunette as she packed her case.

"I thought you wasn't leaving?" Cam asked. Michelle sniffed, continuing to fold and place her clothes in the case that lay open on the bed.

"I thought you didn't care," she replied indifferently, looking up from her task.

"You know I do," Cam said, her voice calm and

confident. Michelle tossed the shirt she was holding into the case and crossed her arms. Her brown eyes that always seemed so alive now looked so sad and distant. *Has she given up?*

"Yes, I know, and yet here I am packing to leave because you have made it abundantly clear that you don't want me here." Her palms faced upwards as she indicated the case on the bed in front of her. Tears threatened to spill out at any moment and it tugged at Cam's heart, her throat constricted.

"I want you to stay," she admitted. "I'm not promising anything, but I would like you to stay and talk." Michelle took a moment to study her, standing stoically by the door with her arms wrapped around herself, before she nodded.

Cam left the room, finally ready to sit down and talk.

Chapter Thirty–Seven

Evening fell and the sun dipped into the sea far out on the horizon, the sky a torrent of burnt oranges and reds, yellow and silver glinting off the water. Even under these circumstances, with her heart hurting the way that it was, Cam still saw the beauty of it all.

She had made a quick pasta dish, while Michelle had unpacked and spent the afternoon in her room under the pretence of taking a nap, though Cam felt she just wanted some space and who could blame her. They both needed this time to sort through their own thoughts and concerns, but now as she placed the dish of cheese-covered pasta into the oven to brown off, she was ready.

She knocked lightly on Michelle's door and let her know that dinner was almost done. Having then laid the table outside with cutlery and plates, she sliced some bread and opened a bottle of red wine to accompany their meal. The pasta was almost ready to come out of the oven when Michelle joined her in the kitchen. A shy smile greeted Cam as she looked up from inspecting the food in the oven.

"Won't be long, why don't you take a seat?"

"It smells wonderful," Michelle said, stepping out through the door and on the patio. Candles lit the area and the sweet smell of citronella hung in the air. The soft chirping of the cicadas was once again the musical backdrop. It was relaxing and peaceful. It would be romantic under any other circumstances.

Michelle poured two large glasses of wine and stood to the edge of the patio. There was a light out at sea, a boat most likely. She heard Cam step outside and move up behind her. There was space between them, but she could still feel her presence. It was magnetic, a heat that drew her in. She wanted to lean back and enjoy it, to bask in its familiarity.

"What made you change your mind?" she asked, grateful she wasn't sitting on a plane heading back to the states right now.

"You love me." It was that simple. Michelle turned to face her and found those blue orbs focused intently on her once more. Gone at last was the icy glare that threatened to freeze her heart forever.

"I do." She took a tentative step forward, and when Camryn didn't back away, she closed the distance completely. Her palm lay flat against Cam's chest. She hadn't touched her like this for weeks, and she savoured it. "I love you Camryn, and I'm not afraid of it or ashamed of it."

"I love you too."

"I know you do, I've never doubted that." Michelle smiled, her palm raised higher to cup Cam's cheek. "Shall we eat?"

~Out~

Bowls empty and bellies full, the wine was flowing. It was a nice evening, warm both in temperature and temperament. Conversation flowed easily between them as they both had, so far, stuck to safer subjects.

"Do you want to tell me about Jessica?" Michelle asked,

the first to brave a more difficult topic. She saw Cam visibly stiffen at the mention of her name and wondered just what this woman had done.

"Do I want to tell you? No," replied Cam, shaking her head. She took a long swig of red wine and swallowed before adding, "But I will." She had decided earlier in the day that she needed to talk about Jessica with Michelle. It was only fair; how did she expect total honesty from her when she wasn't prepared to share her own secrets?

"You don't have to." Michelle smiled, giving her an out.

"Yeah, I do." She smiled nervously. She took a moment, settling herself before she began. "Jessica was my girlfriend. More than that; we lived together, back in London." Michelle listened intently as she refreshed both of their drinks. "It was just before Christmas and I was working, but I'd come down with this really awful cold and my boss sent me home early." She took a sip of her drink, licked her lips and considered her words, deciding it was probably best to just rip off the band aid. "I found her in bed with my best friend." It took a moment for Michelle to catch up and work through exactly what it was that Cam had just said.

"In bed with?"

"My best friend, yes." She downed the last mouthful and placed the glass on the table.

"I don't know what to say? I can't imagine how awful that would be." Not knowing what to say didn't mean she didn't understand her partner a lot better now. The complete betrayal of not just the person she loved, but her best friend too. It didn't bear thinking about. "What did you do?"

"I packed my stuff and left. Dossed on friends' sofas for a while and then found a room in a house-share with some students. It wasn't ideal, but it was all I could afford." She could see that Michelle was struggling with something. "I didn't always have money." She grinned.

"I was trying to work out how you went from sharing a house to living in LA and owning a yacht."

"I'll tell you about that another time. It doesn't matter right now."

Michelle nodded. It really didn't matter to her unless it was by nefarious means, but Cam really didn't strike her as someone who worked for the mob or who was an international jewel thief.

"When I got to LA, I made a decision about dating, and I hurt someone in the process. I didn't mean to, but I hadn't explained myself to her properly, and she thought my dating her meant I wanted a relationship." Cam thought back to Amanda. She only hoped that she hadn't caused her too much hurt. "She slapped me." The blonde rubbed her cheek, reminded of the sharp pain for an instant. "I didn't date anyone for more than one night after that. Until..." Their eyes met and held. "Until I met you." She looked away momentarily, her eyes sweeping upward as though she drew inspiration from the heavens. "I wanted you the moment I saw you. But more than that, I didn't want just a shag. I didn't want to be a memory for you. And that scared me, just as much as you were scared about being outed."

"Why?" she asked. Cam leant across the table, her elbow

resting on the dark wood and supporting her head as she thought how best to word it.

"Do you..." she began, but quickly changed her mind. "Who have you heard me speak about? Like, people in my life." She sat back up and stared at Michelle. The brunette thought about it and shook her head a little.

"I don't know. Erin and Maria, Gavin obviously." Cam was nodding.

"So, my bar manager, my housekeeper and my security manager?" Michelle squinted at her, trying to understand. "I never talk about my family or friends from back home. The only friends I have here work for me or use the bar. Angie and Fran. You." She said the last word so reverently that it almost brought tears to Michelle's eyes. "See, when I let you in here," she tapped the space in her chest where her heart lived, "it was the scariest thing I had done in a long time, scarier than packing up my life and moving 5000 miles away. Scarier than telling my dad to get lost, forgetting that I had a mother that would never stand up for me or a sister that left home the second she could and never looked back." She sucked in a deep breath and licked her lips as she thought about her parents for the first time in a few years.

"Why did you tell your father to get lost?"

"It doesn't matter right now. I don't wanna waste my energy on him. I'm just saying..." She tailed off. The silence, for once, wasn't uncomfortable.

"We both came at this from different directions, but ultimately the same place. We were both scared, but in our own ways we have both pushed past that to get where we are now, right?" Michelle stood and moved around the table to where Cam sat. She squatted down and took Cam's hand in her own. "I am head over heels in love with you and I am not going back to being the person I was, living in fear and pretending I was someone I am not." She kissed Cam's fingers. "And you don't have to be stuck in the past holding onto a relationship hurt that you could do nothing about. This Jessica? She was a fool, but I am grateful to her, because she brought you to me."

Chapter Thirty–Eight

Unsure how, whether by some fluke or magic, they had made it as far as the bedroom. Cam had no real memory of how they had gotten there or when their clothes had started to come off, but as she threw open the first door she came to – Michelle's room – she didn't care. Her only thought was how good it felt to be up close and personal with this woman again and that making it to the bed was imperative. The smell of her perfume in the air was enough to fire her up; having her wrapped around her like this was more arousing than anything she could ever imagine.

Michelle had other ideas, however, and as they almost fell through the door, lips crashing together, she made her move. Her palms pressing firmly against Cam's chest, she forced her backwards, colliding against the wall. She was almost feral in her desire to mark her woman, to regain her place in her bed. She hadn't touched this body in weeks and now she was going to make up for it, make sure that every inch of it was worshipped. Every muscle and sinew was going to be worked and stretched to its capacity. And any memory of anyone else would be wiped away. She hated that Camryn had had someone else in her bed.

She tasted like peach as Michelle swept her tongue up the length of her neck and sucked a lobe into her mouth. A shiver made its way down Cam's arm.

"You have no idea how much I want this, *you*," she husked against Cam's ear. When Cam reached between her thighs and felt just how true that was, she growled. "This is all mine." Her hands stroked Cam's flesh, firm and determined. When Cam attempted to touch her again, she found her hands grasped and held tightly against her side. "No, not yet." Michelle's eyes bore into her, searching. "Who was she?"

"Who was who?" Confusing her thoughts, Cam struggled to focus as Michelle continued to tease her neck and jaw.

"The woman you took to bed." Without any warning, Cam felt her lover's fingers press between her thighs, ramping up the level of teasing. "Was she good?"

"I don't...Who?" Delicious feelings were pulsing through her being. Fingertips playfully moved against her, her hips jerking at the sensations being aroused.

"You know who..." she insisted. She was jealous.

"I...don't...please babe...I need you."

Michelle grinned, her lips ghosting across those of her lover. "Tell me who she was, did you fuck her?"

And then it came to her. She knew who Michelle was talking about, and she was done with being teased.

"Sarah, her name...is Sarah." She reached between them and grasped Michelle's arm, ceasing her movements. "You want to know if I fucked her?" Her stare was intent as she reached for her other arm and grasped that too. She pushed off from the wall and propelled them back. Michelle's knees hit the bed and momentum meant she fell backwards with Camryn on her in an instant. "What do you want to hear? That I did? That I took her back to my bed and did things to her that would make your toes curl?" She held Michelle's hands in her own above her head and dropped her pelvis. The brunette's legs widened as Camryn pressed hard against her, beginning her own torturous teasing. "I didn't."

"She kissed you," Michelle growled, her hips rearing upward under the pressure from Cam as the blonde moved against her.

"Yes, she kissed me. I danced with her." Her hips circled, one way and then the other. "And I took her home, got her naked." Their eyes were still locked together, intense and playful. "And then I thought of you, she looked like you, but she wasn't. She didn't smell like you," she let go of her hands and began to explore the writhing body beneath her, "Or feel like you."

"No, she wasn't me." She gasped as Cam lifted her thigh higher, the pressure against her core intensifying as Cam rocked harder. She threaded her arms around the blonde's neck and tightened her hold. "She could never be me."

~Out~

Chapter Thirty–Nine

When they finally awoke, it was long after midday. The sun beating through the window was hot. They exchanged whispered good mornings and brief kisses before even opening their eyes. It amazed Cam just how easily they could fall back into the comfortable relationship that they had. There was no pretending it hadn't happened, but it was dealt with, a line drawn, and for both of them it meant moving forward.

"We should get up and enjoy what is left of the day, don't ya think?" Michelle asked.

"Nope, we should stay here where we can shag for the rest of the day." Cam laughed as she rolled over and pinned her giggling lover to the bed.

"Camryn you are insatiable!" she said, before responding to her kiss.

~Out~

Yawning and stretching out limbs that had, for the most part, been given no real respite in the preceding 18 hours meant that everything ached as Cam clambered out of bed and walked naked to the bathroom.

Michelle couldn't help but admire the toned musculature of Cam's body. *And she says I have a remarkable body.*

Hearing the shower switch on, Michelle smiled to herself and followed. Her muscles aching too, she wandered across the hall to the bathroom and leant on the door jamb, watching.

"Need any help in there?"

"No, but I don't mind sharing anyway." Cam smiled and opened the glass door to the shower cubicle, making room for her partner to slip in under the water beside her.

For once there was nothing sexual other than the intimacy of sharing a small, wet space in close proximity. They washed each other's hair and soaped each other's bodies as the steam built up around them, and discussed the idea of swimming and relaxing by the pool with some lunch, and maybe later going into town for some entertainment. For Cam it didn't matter what they did; she just wanted to stay close, to be connected and enjoy being in love again.

~Out~

Once dried off and dressed (as dressed as you can be in swimsuits and towels), they made their way to the garden and the pool area. Cam was laden with a tray of goodies to nibble on, whilst Michelle carried a bottle of wine and a bag of essentials. Neither of them wanted to move once they were settled. It was glorious and hot; summer was coming to an end and yet the weather held. She watched Michelle get settled and then reach for the sun lotion. Spraying her arms and then her legs, she rubbed the cream in. A mischievous idea popped in to the blonde's head.

"Sit forward and I'll do your back for you." She smiled, moving to take a seat straddled behind her lover on the lounger.

"Thank you." She returned the smile and passed the

238

bottle of lotion behind her to Cam's waiting hands. The blonde lifted her hair away and proceeded to spray her shoulders and bare back, giggling as Michelle jumped to the feeling of the cool liquid. Cam's warm palms spread the cream around, covering every inch. Slowly she tugged at the strings holding the bikini top in place. Michelle said nothing as the ones around her neck loosened and fell forwards, Cam's fingertips replacing them as she soothed the cream into her skin. And then Cam untied the other strings that held firm around her midriff.

"Cam!" she shrieked, as the blonde whipped the flimsy material away. Michelle's arms covered her chest in an instant.

"What? Nobody can see us up here." She took hold of her lover's arms and slowly prised them away, revealing her chest to the sunshine. With a quick spray of lotion, her hands encapsulated her breasts and covered them with the appropriate sunscreen. She took her time and enjoyed the feeling of soft skin beneath her palms, her nipples hardening to the sensation and the daring exposure.

The property was completely free from being overlooked by anyone. You would have to be out at sea on a boat with a telescopic lens and know they were there to capture anything as juicy as Shelly Hamlin with her boobs out, kissing her lesbian lover.

"Wanna get naked, sunbathe the European way?" Cam whispered against the shell of her ear. Goosebumps rose in an instant. Michelle nodded, lifted her ass, and tugged her bottoms off, dropping them to the patio. Being with this woman was freeing and she loved every minute of it.

Chapter Forty

As evening fell, they took a walk along the beach. The sun dipped low beyond the horizon, leaving the sky streaked from blue to orange; eventually it would turn to black. There was a light breeze and the beach was almost empty. Tourists and locals had all packed up for the day, leaving only the sun worshippers clinging onto the very last vestiges of light. Michelle shivered a little and Cam wrapped her jacket around her shoulders and pulled her in closer, enjoying the feeling of being able to touch her like this. They were in public, and yet nobody took any notice of them.

"I just thought, other than Erin, does anyone actually know where you are right now?!"

Michelle's hand flew to her mouth and she stopped dead in her tracks. "Oh my God, I didn't even think." She laughed. "Janice probably has a manhunt looking for me."

"Maybe you should give her a call when we get back, it's still early in LA."

"Yes, I will. She is going to kick my ass though."

"Well, if she does, I promise to kiss it better." Cam winked and smiled at the thought, her arm passing around her shoulder again, kissing her temple. "In fact, I'll do that anyway"

A little further along the beach, they stopped to pick up shells and pebbles, launching them into the waves and competing to see how far they could throw them. The charcoal smell of barbeque wafted in the air as the numerous restaurants set up for the evening's dining.

"So, are you ready to go home yet?" Cam asked as her next effort skipped along the top of the calm water, smooth and flat as it chipped at the water's surface three, then four times.

"I came here to be with you. If you want to stay, I stay. If you want to go then I go, that's how simple it is for me." Although she knew eventually she would need to go home. She was contracted to so many things that it was near impossible to get out of them all without going bankrupt and becoming unemployable. Interviews could be rejigged, even her time on *Medical Diaries* could be adjusted for a short break such as an illness, but she would have to return.

"I came here to escape you!" Cam laughed and nudged her shoulder just as she was about to pitch her own pebble.

"How's that working out for ya?" The brunette laughed and gently pushed her for ruining the shot, but Cam grabbed her easily and pulled her close.

"I could never have escaped you, because you're in here." Cam breathed in the night air, salty and warm. She brought Michelle's and her own hands together and placed them over her heart. Warm water lapped at their feet as they kissed, publicly and uncaring.

~Out~

"Janice, hey it's me." Michelle spoke into the phone as Cam made her own call home to speak with Erin.

"Michelle, where are you? I tried to call you but your phone isn't working."

She was laid out on their bed listening, but she could also hear Cam walking around the house as she had her own conversation. Picturing the blonde blushing slightly as she admitted that Erin was right. She smiled to herself as she realised that fact too.

"Yeah, I turned it off." Her phone was never off. She tried to focus better on Janice, but it was difficult when just the sound of Camryn speaking was enough to send her arousal levels into hyperspace.

"Have you got ya head together now? Did you speak to Cam?"

"I did." Janice didn't need to hear any more to know that Michelle was now much happier. She could hear the smile that was languidly turning up the corners of her client's mouth.

"Good, I am glad. Now, I need you in the office tomorrow," Janice said firmly. Someone had to put some reality on the table, and that was her job!

"Ah, that might be a problem," Michelle answered, chewing her lip. "I am in Greece."

There was silence on the phone. She sat up and pulled the device away from her ear to check they hadn't been disconnected.

"I am sorry, I thought for a minute you said Greece," Janice chuckled. "Can you say that again?"

"You heard correctly. I'm in Greece with Camryn." She lay back down on the bed and thought about that. *With Camryn.*

"Michelle, I know I am the best at what I do, but what the hell are you doing in Greece? I can hold the wolves at bay for so long, but you need to be here so we can start planning how we go forward with this."

"I know and I promise, I'll be back as soon as I can."

~Out~

"All ok?" Cam asked, receiving a kiss. She was sitting at the dressing table brushing her hair. Her call with Erin had ended on a happy note; with Erin clearly off the hook for her part in bringing them back together, she was quietly impressed that her friend had had the balls to do what she did, knowing she risked her job.

"Yes, though she would prefer it if I was to get on the first flight home." Michelle's fingers began to play with Cam's hair as Cam put the brush down and leant back into the touch.

"Do you want to go home?" Cam inquired through the mirror, her eyes closed as she enjoyed Michelle's work.

"No but, we're going to have to at some point, right? Face the music."

"I guess so, I can get it organised if you'd like?" Cam said openly, not wanting to cause any further trouble for Michelle. Whatever happened from now on, she accepted that Michelle needed her privacy and her career.

"I don't *like*, I mean, I like this bubble we're in," she said, tugging her fingers through all of Cam's locks and tying them high up on her head in a ponytail.

"Me too, but we will have to leave at some point." Their

eyes met in the mirror. A silent exchange of acceptance was shared. Life would soon go back to normal.

"I know, do you think things will change?" Michelle asked, letting her arms fall around Cam's shoulders, her lips kissing her neck when the blonde tilted her head to the side.

"I think that things will be different, yes. We will have to be more careful around other people, but once the door is closed, I don't see how anything has to change," she said, enjoying the attention.

"As much as I really like doing this right now, I need to shower and change!" Michelle sighed.

"Ok. Skedaddle, I'll meet you in bed," Cam said, rising and kissing her mouth.

Cam climbed into bed, naked as usual, setting her pillows upright so she could read her book for a few minutes until her bed mate returned. She was comfortable as she read about the exploits of a detective and her medical examiner friend on the case of a psychopath. She had the windows closed and the air conditioning unit on low in an effort to avoid any further insect bites.

When Michelle finished her shower, she quickly dried off and threw on the first thing she found. As she opened the door to the bedroom, Cam looked up and was dumbstruck to see Michelle in just a shirt, her shirt, buttoned up to mid-chest. Long tanned legs that seemed to go on forever slowly made their way further into the room, fingers slowly unfastening buttons, her gaze never leaving Cam's face as she watched her lover's eyes darken with desire.

"Jesus, do they teach you this stuff in acting school?" she said as she placed her book in the bedside cabinet, still not taking her eyes off Michelle.

"Actually, they do! But, when I'm with you, I don't ever..." She reached the last button. "Ever..." the shirt fell open, revealing her bare torso as she climbed knee first on the bed, "Ever! Feel the need to act."

Cam reached up, took her face in her hands and brought their lips together, as their bodies closed the gap and flesh met flesh once more.

"How about for the next thirty minutes or so, you just let me be the director and you try and remember your lines?" She grinned and twisted, getting herself comfortable, moving lower down the bed.

Chapter Forty-One

It took two more days before they were ready to leave and take the long flight back to the states. Gavin collected them at the airport and drove them straight to Cam's place on the beach. They figured they could at least pretend they were still in Greece if they could hear the waves and walk along the sand.

"Maria?" Cam called out as they all but fell through the door. Tired from the long journey, she dropped her case in the hallway and Michelle followed suit, unsure what else she should do.

"Always with the shouting Camryn. Why you got to shout all the time?" Maria said, smiling as she came into view and looked her over, making sure she was in one piece. She looked good: no bags under her eyes, tanned and glowing. She was sober! Maria felt her heart lift.

"I have to shout because I can never find you," Cam said, wrapping her arms around the woman she had come to love and respect. She had missed her, forgiven her already.

"That's because I spend all day cleaning up your mess," she said with a serious face. "And who is this?" she asked. Looking to Michelle, she smiled. She knew who she was and was pleased that Erin's plan had worked.

"Hi, I'm Michelle." She smiled, reaching a hand out.

"Ah the elusive Michelle," Maria said, taking the proffered hand and shaking hard. "It's about time."

~Out~

It took an hour to unpack with Cam insisting that Michelle use her wardrobe to place her clothes. She cleared space in a drawer and made room on the dresser for all of Michelle's things. She chuckled internally as she realised she had gone from someone not willing to date more than once to someone more than eager to share her space with her girlfriend.

~Out~

"Oh my god," Cam exclaimed as she fell backwards onto the couch. "The only thing I hate about living here is how bloody far it is to visit Europe. I'm knackered!"

"It is a tiring journey but..." Michelle sat on Cam's lap, wrapping her arms around her neck. "We made the most of it, so was it worth it?" Michelle smirked like the cat that got the cream, thinking back to the long flight home and how she was now a fully paid up member of the Mile High Club, several times over. Having a private jet fly you home made for a lot of opportunities, and Cam had been insistent that they take them while they could. She would never be able to look at a leather recliner again without recalling the way Cam had tilted it back just as Michelle was on the verge of climax, the movement allowing her a deeper, harder thrust that had had the brunette blaspheming for a full minute. She was also pretty sure the imprint of Cam's butt would forever be visible on the shiny mahogany unit where she had perched, impaled by Michelle as her digits went to work.

"Yes, it was definitely worth it."

~Out~

Michelle called Janice again and made arrangements for

a meeting with her agent the following day. They agreed that it would be easier for Janice to come to the beach to avoid anyone spotting Cam and Michelle entering her building. She shared offices with other agents and people in the business, so it was always a spot being haunted by paparazzi and reporters hoping to bag a headline. The last thing they needed right now was for Michelle to be outed. That would be her choice, not the press's.

Cam leant against the door jamb listening to the conversation. Michelle turned, phone to her ear still as she listened to Janice speaking. She winked at Cam and mouthed 'I love you'. She looked relaxed and carefree as she stood there.

They had come a long way in such a short space of time. Cam's rule of never falling in love had been well and truly tossed out of the window the minute Michelle Hamilton walked through the door of Out.

Right now, Camryn Thomas was in love, and whatever life had to throw at her from now on, she would embrace it. Things had changed, gone her way, she was sure of it.

To be continued...

If you have enjoyed OUT

Here is a taste of Claire Highton-Stevenson's next book in the Camryn Thomas series.

Coming soon

Camryn Thomas and Michelle Hamilton have finally got their life heading in the right direction. Together.

But even when you're happy, life will throw up some curve balls.

How will they deal with the idea of Michelle coming Out?

And what will happen when they discover that somebody isn't happy about their relationship at all?

Get ready to find out what happens 'Next!'

Chapter One

When Janice Rashbrook arrived at dead on 10 a.m. as planned, she entered in a whirlwind of authority; this wasn't a woman who took any prisoners! With her power suit and briefcase, she was the epitome of Hollywood hardcore. What she hadn't seen, heard, or talked about wasn't worth knowing.

"So, lovebirds, let's talk, and while we're at it, I'll have a coffee, black, no sugar!" she demanded, not requested. Cam raised an eyebrow at Michelle and received a shrug and a smirk in return.

Cam could hear the conversation while she set up the coffee machine and gathered some mugs. There really was nothing nicer than the smell of fresh coffee brewing as far as Cam was concerned. Her place was much like Michelle's: open-planned and spacious, with a lot of light streaming in from the windows and doors that faced the beach. Her kitchen, although a separate room, was just feet from where Michelle sat elegantly with Janice by her side.

"First we need to decide, are you in or out?"

"Huh?" said Michelle, her attention stuck firmly on Camryn's butt. The blonde seemed to have found some kind of rhythm in her head as she tensed each cheek. It was almost hypnotising as each cheek lifted and fell.

"Out!! Ya know, of the closet...no longer in Narnia, cruising the strip!" Janice used up her entire repertoire of LGBT retorts as Cam turned to join them in the room, carrying a tray of hot coffees, completely oblivious to the attention her girlfriend had been paying her.

"She means are you telling the world you're a lesbian," Cam deadpanned before grinning. She liked Janice. They sat on the same board for an arts foundation Cam was involved with and often had a giggle at someone else's expense. Though neither were ever mean or nasty, they couldn't help but see the humour in a lot of the things that went on in LA; it was a crazy place at times.

"Oh, uh...well, what happens if I wanted to come out? Officially? I mean people already know, so..." she inquired of her agent. She thanked Cam as she passed her a mug of hot coffee.

"Well first off, we get you booked on Ellen," she sniggered. The opportunity to play a little more with her client was just too much to ignore, especially as she clearly had Camryn's approval.

"Ha ha." A snarky reply came from Michelle, but she grinned anyway. "Could we take this seriously maybe?"

Cam smiled from her vantage point. She loved Michelle in all her guises, but she had a real soft spot for when she got a little riled.

"Ok seriously, I don't think there will be any issue with *MD*, they have several gay cast members already and have had two gay characters so far, so I don't foresee any problems there. And it's been a pretty closed set in terms of gossip leaking, so I'm not worried."

"Ok well that's good." Michelle breathed a sigh of relief.

"But." She held up a finger. "It will probably stifle any

prospective film parts. Right now you still get cast as the eye candy; once it's out that you're 'out,' the money men might be less likely to cast you as they do now!"

"Why?" Cam asked as she picked up her mug and sipped the dark nectar. "She's an actress, she got cast as a doctor without being one, why is there such an issue with playing straight sex sirens?"

"Because dear Camryn, the real world is full of assholes!" Never one to shy away from the truth, she wasn't going to start now. "And we haven't even got to the fans yet."

"Fair enough, but it's still not fucking right."

"Ok, so what about if we keep it quiet?" Michelle asked, resting her hand on Cam's leg.

"Well then it depends on how quiet you plan to be, silent? Nothing much changes. Out to colleagues? Again, no real change to your employment. However, bigger risk of some asshole outing ya, but it's down to you Shelly. This is your career; it's you that's going to have to make the decision, and the fact that you say people already know may mean you have no choice."

Janice and Camryn both gave their attention fully to Michelle. She looked between each of them and then burst into tears!

"I don't know!" she cried. "What do I do?" Cam quickly placed her coffee down on the table and reached for her, guiding her into a hug that protected her from all the horribleness outside.

"Janice is right, this has to be your choice, but for now we stay silent and give you time to decide." Cam spoke the words carefully, needing Michelle to know this was all okay.

"Really? You don't want me to come out and acknowledge you?"

"What I want is for *you* to be happy and for *you* to acknowledge me. I don't need your fans to accept me or for your boss to like me. I just don't want you to feel ashamed of what we have."

"I'm not, I promise you I am not ashamed of you or of us but, this is my dream! It has been my whole life, to act and be an actor. I don't want to give that up and it's not fair that I have to consider not being able to do what I love just to be happy like anyone else." She picked at imaginary fluff on Cam's jumper, an overwhelming need developing inside her to just lock herself away in a room with only Camryn for company, where they could make love and be together without the pressures and judgement of the world.

"Life ain't fair honey, never has been. Like I said, I can keep this quiet, but you're going to have to get ya head around the idea that one misplaced hand—" she nodded towards Michelle's hand on Camryn's leg, "kiss, or word, and you could be outed."

"You said that some people can come out and make it work for them. So, why can't it work for me?" she spoke to Janice.

"It can, but it would mean possibly doing what I said earlier. Taking parts that are different from the ones you do now. It means advertising might drop off. You'll have to deal with the press and go on every talk show that asks. Put up with fans making comments you might not like to read."

"I don't care about the money Jan, I have enough money, it's never been about the money!" she said, looking to Cam who held her hand still.

"You say that now, but you've got a lifestyle you enjoy, and that costs money!" Janice emphasised.

"I have money, it's not an issue," Cam announced.

"Really?" Janice turned and looked right at Cam. "And what happens if this is just a little phase or you two have a fight like you've just had and decide not to be together anymore, what then? She gives up her whole career and you get to walk away. She has to live with any choice she makes now!" Janice glared at Cam. She liked the Brit, but at the end of the day she was paid to do what was best for Michelle, and what was best for Michelle was best for her too.

"We're not going to break up," Michelle whispered.

"You don't know that!" Janice replied gently.

"She's right, all the risk is on you Michelle, your entire life is going to change because of me!" Cam shrugged, realising just how much life could change for them both.

"Then so be it, I know what I want!"

"Do you? We haven't left this bubble for ten days. People already know, and as much as I trust them, all that it takes is one stupid comment to the wrong person. Once it's common knowledge, there is no taking it back."

"Ok Cam I get it, ok!" Michelle said sharply before she blew out a breath and checked her anger. She wasn't angry with Cam or Janice; it was the situation. How dare the world be so difficult just because she fell in love? "I'm sorry, I don't mean to shout, it's not your fault."

"I will support you in any decision you make. I'll walk 50 feet behind you to avoid a photograph, I'll stay home while you go on a 'date' with some stud from the studio, I'll keep on planning secret dates for us to enjoy in private, or I'll hold your hand with pride and stand on the red carpet with you; I'll do interviews and let them print any crap they like about me, but you have to decide which it is." She reached her hand for her lover once more and kissed her fingertips.

Michelle looked to Janice and said, "You see why I love her?"

"Oh I'm very aware of Camryn's attributes, Shelly. Look let's leave things as they are, you two stay in your little bubble for a few more days and come up with an answer. I need to get going. Oh and Michelle, Saturday you have a charity event to attend, I'll text you the details later but you will need a date so, let's just say that whoever you turn up with will be the answer."

Cam saw her to the door, and when she returned she found Michelle still sitting on the sofa, her legs tucked up underneath her. Cam sat down, and Michelle climbed into her lap and curled up.

"Why does it have to be so hard? All I want is to do my job and love you, is that too much to ask?"

"No, in the real world it wouldn't really make any

difference, but you are a story. Who knows, other actresses have come out, and the media doesn't hassle them."

"I just don't know if I want to live my entire life as a lie."

"You wouldn't be, we wouldn't be a lie at home, we would be able to tell our friends and family and enjoy a limited amount of freedom still."

"But why should we? I know I'm new to all this but I hate it, I hate that I have to hide you."

Cam smiled. How things had changed in just a few weeks. Michelle had gone from wanting to hide herself to now being angered by it, and Cam went from being out and proud to wanting to protect her lover with whatever it took, even if that meant pretending she didn't exist.

"I just think maybe things will work out," Michelle said. "We can keep our life private and still be a regular couple."

"Maybe, we still need to be careful though baby." Cam placed her hands on Michelle's waist and pulled her into her. She needed to make sure that she wasn't getting ahead of herself. "We can go out and do normal things, but we still have to keep our hands to ourselves just in case."

"I know," she whined, a little disappointed. "I just, I really love just being with you and doing normal everyday boring stuff."

"Good cos, I have *so* many really boring normal things for you to do, starting with the hoovering." She grinned.

"The what?"

"Vacuuming love, vacuuming!! The place needs cleaning, so let's get moving." She laughed at the look on Michelle's face. There was never going to be any cleaning needed doing in this house, not with Maria here anyway, but it was fun to mess with her a little.

"You seriously want to spend this evening cleaning house?"

"No I don't, that's why I have Maria, but she has the afternoon off and you said you wanted to do all the boring—"

She was cut off before she could finish by Michelle's lips crushing hers. "You are a bad, bad woman Camryn, making your girlfriend clean house when you should be making love to her."

"Oh now you don't want to do the boring things no?"

"You are such a funny woman. Now strip!" Michelle demanded.

If she thought sweet and lovely Michelle was sexy as hell, then Cam was completely undone by demanding and confident Michelle!

"You want me to strip?" she said, standing with a mischievous glint in her eye.

"Pretty sure that's what I said, you didn't seem to have a problem with it in the parking lot at OUT." She licked her lip before biting the lower one between her teeth. One leg crossed over the other, Michelle sat back and got herself comfortable for the show.

"I see," Cam said, as she wandered over to the Bose

sound system and flicked through some CDs, picking out the one she wanted. As the music kicked in and the bass picked up, she turned and locked eyes with Michelle, her hips started to sway as she reached up to the first button on her shirt, opening it as she sashayed towards Michelle who sat open-mouthed at this impromptu strip show.

By the time she had crossed the room, dipping, swaying and twisting to the music, she had two more buttons undone. She pushed Michelle backwards with a firm hand on her chest until she was sitting on the couch, wide eyed and amazed.

"No touching," Cam stated, her lap dance commencing with a grin.

ABOUT THE AUTHOR

Claire Highton–Stevenson is a first-time novelist. She grew up in London and subsequently now lives in West Sussex along with her wife and fur babies.

Ambitiously, she tries to travel as much as possible. Maybe a lottery win would help with that! Surprisingly, Los Angeles is high on her list of places to visit.

Claire also enjoys photography, watching her favorite football team and lunching with friends.

Printed in Great Britain
by Amazon

40690096R00145